DEATH MACHINES OF DEATH

FOR KEVIN SHAMEL

DEATH MACHINES OF DEATH

VINCE KRAMER

ERASERHEAD PRESS

ERASERHEAD PRESS
205 NE BRYANT
PORTLAND, OR 97211

WWW.ERASERHEADPRESS.COM

ISBN: 978-1-62105-116-9

Copyright © 2013 by Vince Kramer

Cover art copyright © 2013 Hauke Vagt

Printed in the USA.

AUTHOR'S NOTE:

Vodka + Orange Juice
Batteries
ADULT Iguana Food
(check to see if Desmond
is four-feet-long yet)
Googly Eyes
Beer
Gummi Bears
Crimson Typhoon
Action figure
New Carcass CD
McDonald's
Longest screwdriver
they have at
Wal-Mart
Oil Change

PROLOGUE CHAPTER

Stephen King's guts flew everywhere. He screamed as he was ripped apart. Torrents of his own blood splashed across his face and blinded his terrorized eyes.

He had tried to escape. He'd made it pretty far too, limping down his driveway with an extension cord wrapped around his leg, dragging a smashed electric knife with it. It had cut through his tendons and tried to kill him, just like the kitchen blender had somehow shred his wife to pieces. It was like every machine in the house had come to life. His children were killed by a combination of televisions, stereos, and ceiling fans.

His own Kindle had even tried to kill him, even though he told it not to. "You can't kill *me!*" he said, 'Don't you know who I am?! I'm *Stephen fucking King, goddamnit!*"

But it didn't listen. It was like there was no stopping it!

A gigantic machine hauled itself down the driveway as his six-million-dollar mansion exploded behind it, shooting splintered wood and fireballs in every direction. The whole scene was what one of his books would look like if it were directed by Michael Bay. The machine's body was a grotesque and mangled amalgam of classic cars, lawnmowers, and chainsaws. Its head was the world's LOUDEST STEREO (because Stephen King owned that). Its neck was a large jukebox, full of the soundtracks to every Stephen King movie. It shot a never-ending supply of CDs out of its mouth.

Stephen King had the soundtrack to *The Shining* sticking in his back.

The sinister machine's arms were mangled vehicles from

his huge classic car collection swinging chainsaws wildly in every direction. The tractors that made up its legs skittered maniacally on screaming lawnmowers.

It was upon Stephen King before he made it to the end of the driveway. It stopped, and cocked its "head" down at him as the Master of Horror cowered before it. Then it spoke to him.

It said, "Sometimes dead is better."

And then it absolutely killed him to death.

SPACE: THE FIRST CHAPTER

"SPACE NEWS! De-da-de-da-na-nana! SPACE NEWS!" The newscasters sang along with their show's intro, as if infected by some kind of space madness. Which they were, because they had been in space for quite some time and it was infecting them with madness. But don't worry—it's not contagious. You'd have to be in space to catch that kind of madness.

A slick handsome bastard of a newsman swung around in his chair like an overly-excited retard. He stared into the camera, and said, "WELCOME TO SPACE NEWS! News from space, IN space, about space, and about YOU!"

"YES! NEWS IN OUTER SPACE!" the other newscaster screamed.

"IT'S CRAZY!" shouted the first newscaster. He slightly composed himself, shuffled some papers on the news-desk, and whispered to his co-anchor, "It's so cool we're in space, dude."

"I know, I love it so much," the other replied.

"Now tonight's top story! A gigantic comet is hurtling between the Earth and the Moon! It's huge and it's on fire and it looks CRAZY!"

"Yes!" the co-anchor smiled, "and we moved our space station out of the way just in time! It's ROCKET-POWERED! WHOOOOO!"

The other newsman continued, "Scientists believe that the effects of the comet might render all electronic equipment on Earth powerless for the coming week. But not ours! Our space station has a FORCE FIELD!"

"It's the best thing ever!"

9

"The planet Earth will be in the tail of the comet for the following seven days. We'll see what happens, but I wouldn't worry. We survived 2012, so *I'm pretty sure* we're going to survive this." He smirked. "And with more about technology, here's our news correspondent Sally Dreier with a story about it! Sally?"

A young blonde newswoman appeared on the screen wearing a yellow trenchcoat and holding a microphone up to her ear. "Is technology making us *retarded?* Yes. I feel so stupid, all the time, and I still can't get enough of it. Oh my god, I'm just so retarded. Back to you, Steve!"

Then the space station/news station/glorified piece of space-junk exploded, killing everyone onboard instantly.

It apparently had *not* moved out of the way of the comet.

CHAPTER RETARDS

Kevin was sick of it all: His job, his cats, his overwhelmingly depressing life full of crushing loneliness and despair. It was killing him. He couldn't remember the last time he had energy. The time when he used to get laid now seemed like it was in another life. He hated his memories of that life. They hurt him. Things had been so stagnant and boring for so long.

Sometimes, when his mad thoughts got the best of him, he shouted to himself, "I'm not real!" without wanting to. As insane as that was, it felt accurate. It kind of just summed it all up. The compulsion of having to say that aloud several times a day was disturbing. He knew that.

Recently, Kevin got his first gray hair. He flipped out, and it sent him headfirst into a midlife crisis. It was terrifying, but on the other hand, it was the first new thing that had happened to him in a long time. It was a *change*. It made him think about his life, and for the first time since he could remember, he wanted to do something about it.

He put the hair in a sandwich bag, drank a case of beer, and stared at it. And he *thought*. He thought and thought. About things he had never thought about before, or had just chosen to ignore. It killed him, and he didn't like that. It was almost like it made him angry enough to actually do something about it for once.

A change. And that word that had always been far beyond him—action.

After a few days of sleep, Kevin got online and started searching for something to do. *Something* he could do. And it turned out *anything* could be *something*. It was almost mystifying, reading about all of these things and the flashes of fantasy that shot through his mind of *actually doing them*. He felt beneath it, but still willing to try it. He had read something recently about, "Openness to Experience", and how the people that carried that personality trait were actually a lot happier than most people. He had always wanted to be that way. But he was too scared. He worried about even leaving the house. His cats might die, or he might die, someone might break into his house and steal all of his stuff and kill his cats, or the house might catch on fire, killing his cats and destroying all of his stuff and then he might die.

This was going to be a big step for Kevin.

He looked at his gray hair he had put in the plastic bag, which was always with him. And he thought, *What does it matter?*

He signed up for something. He committed to it. He pressed send. He had a few days to figure out how he was going to leave his house behind for an afternoon. He was going to venture out there, into the unknown, and see what it held.

He was going to prove that he was real.

Amy had puked all over her tits again.

She awoke to jackhammers in her brain, due in part to the relentless landscaping going on outside at such an ungodly hour. And also her long night of binge drinking and debauchery.

The lawnmowers screamed and the leaf-blowers roared as unbearable heat beamed through her windows torturously. It was that time of the month, *the worst time*, when the landscapers came to do their job.

On these days, she always wished she had marked it on the calendar. One day she wished she could do that. Be prepared. Maybe not drink the night before. Or get a hotel for the week. Or get into the kind of lifestyle where she woke up at the crack of dawn, drank a protein shake or something and went for a long morning jog, all happy like the person you're supposed to be. Some kind of stupid fantasy like that.

She couldn't remember how many guys she had blown the night before. She was supposed to be keeping track, so she could break her previous record. Then she thought hard—recounting. Six? Pretty good for one night. But then she remembered only four of them had cum in her mouth, which really is the most important part. So, it was meaningless. She had failed. But she was so close. She knew she could do better.

Amy tore off her puke-spattered t-shirt and looked at herself in the mirror. She frowned. She was bloated and filthy. She punched the mirror, screaming, *"Fuck you!"* She almost started crying, but then said, "I don't have time for this shit!"

She turned on the shower and went to make a cup of coffee, so the water would be hot by the time she got in. When she did, she masturbated, thinking, *Today's the day. Today's the day I blow more guys than I ever have in my life.* Only then, did she think she would be truly happy.

When she went to her room to get dressed, a Mexican with a chainsaw, rapelling down the tree outside of her window, saw her naked and accidentally fell to his death.

Jordy was ECSTATIC! Like every morning, he knew that *this* was going to be the best day of his life. He was the most popular kid in school, excelled in every sport, and absolutely *everyone ever* was his best friend. *EVERYONE* loved him. He was the best person *EVER*. He looked in the mirror, smiled, wiped the drool from his mouth, and went, *"YAY! I'm the best person EVER!"* Then he put on his helmet and ran out of the house screaming *"YAAAAAAY!!! JORDY!!!!"*

Jordy was retarded.

And people in modern society are very nice.

A hundred and eighty years old and still horny as hell. What is wrong with me? Robert frowned as he looked at himself nude in the mirror. He had an erection. It had happened somewhere between getting out of the shower and drying off without him even realizing it. But senior citizens don't even need to be thinking about sex to get an erection. It is in this way that they are like children—that and pooping their pants.

Robert probably wasn't a hundred and eighty years old, but he'd heard that he was so many times that he was starting to believe it. Many other things said about him were also probably not true, but he almost didn't even know which things were anymore, or have the spirit to care. It all seemed pointless at his ripe old age of one-eighty. And his life had been great; a full one, he'd heard. When he was eighteen he was in the Civil War, and conquered it.

When he thought back he could almost remember it like it had actually happened. He was also ten feet tall and stopped a Martian invasion with his bare hands. He thought that must be where the scar on his stomach came from. Back then he could kill a man just by looking at him.

Robert tried this sometimes, and he got pretty depressed because he simply couldn't do it anymore. He figured he must be getting too old. That had to be it. He needed to stop being old somehow so he could kill people with his evil glare again.

Robert spent the next hour masturbating and flexing in the mirror. He was a sexy conqueror god and he was going to stop being old no matter what.

14

"I hate you," said Dan.

"But I *loooove* you." Dave made kissing sounds at him and grabbed his crotch.

Dan grabbed his hand and removed it. "Don't touch me there! And get out of bed with me!"

Dave frowned and yelled, "FINE!"

"We better get ready. Today is important."

"But I just had a great new idea! If we like, just take photos of things standing upside-down, but then print them out right-side-up, it will be the biggest thing to sweep the art world since that retard painted shit with his left foot!"

Dan sighed. "Maybe, but not today. This is going to be worth going to. Now let's get in the shower."

Dave could not stop touching himself in the shower, and trying to grab Dan's penis. It was going to take much longer than usual unless he let Dave have his way with him, so he let him have at it so they could move on, get it over with, and get ready.

"Ah, that felt so good. Didn't that feel good, Dan?" Dave smiled at Dan from the mirror, doing his tie wrong.

"Stop that! You're doing it wrong." Dan grabbed the tie from Dave and took over, making it PERFECT—a concept that seemed far out of Dave's grasp.

"You look good." Dave commented, and gave him a wink.

"*WE* look good. Now come on, let's get out of here before we're late."

Dan/Dave put on his shoes (one sock, one shoe at a time), grabbed his keys and jacket and walked out the door.

He was back a minute later to check the appliances because Dave convinced him they were all on, then he grabbed his crotch again.

Andrew was one of the most artistic kids on the block. He was talented in many areas, including music, art, and poetry.

He was also *autistic*, so all the other kids called him a fucking retard all the time. To which he would always reply, "You are talking to me. You are my friend." So, Andrew just thought he had a lot of friends.

The Centers for Disease Control (CDC for short) had been putting up flyers all over the neighborhood, warning that individuals with autism and other disabilities were dangerous. There was a number on the flyer to call if you saw anyone acting in a suspiciously retarded manner, and the CDC would pick them up and take them to a mental reassignment class.

Andrew had taken down every flyer in the neighborhood. He'd noticed various errors and spelling mistakes and fixed them, then put each and every one back exactly where he had found them. The new "TCFDC" flyers urged people to report anyone acting in a suspiciously *mentally challenged* manner, and also included Andrew's full name, address, and phone number to call if they wanted a new friend.

Andrew had just finished writing an exquisite new piano piece, and was on the floor in the kitchen stacking everything from the cabinets into well-organized towers. Authorities from The Centers for Disease Control kicked the door open, seized him and dragged him away. He did not protest in the slightest, excited about how many new friends he suddenly had.

Blaine was in a good mood. An *extremely* good mood. He was on a total high. He had spent the whole morning calling The Centers for Disease Control and telling them the name and address of everyone he'd ever met that had been a total dick to him. He was sure to add explicit details about how they were maniacally retarded in the most violent way possible.

The person that had taken his lunch out of the fridge at work and eaten it was now a child-molesting dog-kicker. His ex-girlfriend who cheated on him was now a dog-molesting child-killer. And so on.

Blaine had been so sad the day before, about all the shit things people had done to him. He felt suicidal, dwelling on it so much. But with the dawn of the new day, he felt GREAT, ready to take on the whole world! Holy shit, life was fucking awesome! The extreme ups and downs of being bipolar—at least the *ups*—made it all worthwhile.

His brother Kevin had emailed him all about this singles mixer for people with mono he was attending at a local resort, which he always thought was some kind of big gay bar because of its name. But he found out online that it *wasn't*, and there was actually some other awesome shit to go to there. He was *totally* going to go check some things out and then hang out with his brother and get wasted.

It was going to be the best day *EVER!*

Sean was gay. He was gay and his name was Sean.
    NEXT!

Jesus was a dick. He thought he was the center of the whole world. Because he was an asshole (and happened to have Asperger's Syndrome).

Chip was crippled, but that wasn't going to stop him. He stopped his wheelchair in front of the refrigerator and put the song, *Nothing's Gonna Stop Us Now,* by Starship up on his iPod. The cookie jar might be out of reach, but those cookies would be his! By the time the song was over the refrigerator and all of its contents were all over the floor. The fridge had almost crushed him to death, but he got out of the way just in time. The cookie jar landed on his lap, the top flew off, and cookies shot all over his chest and face.

He had won.

Nothing ever got Chip down. His father used to call him a little Pollyanna. He would always scream at him, "HEY, LITTLE POLLYANNA! WHY ARE YOU SMILING? YOU HAVE NOTHING TO SMILE ABOUT!" And then he would beat the crap out of him. One time his father beat him so hard with a baseball bat that his spine broke and he became paralyzed. But Chip didn't let that get him down. He looked on the bright side. Wheelchairs are awesome. He wouldn't have to walk anywhere anymore. He put fun stickers on the back.

His father didn't get it. He thought he had just beat his son so hard that he became retarded from it. And since beating him any further definitely wasn't going to make him *less* retarded, Chip's father decided to look at other options.

But Chip wasn't retarded. He was special. A sticker on his wheelchair said so.

CHAPTER
CONVENTIONS

"Christ, doesn't this book have enough characters already? I can't even keep up with who's who anymore. And when the hell are we going to get to the action? What garbage," the desk clerk said, and without hesitation, threw the new Stephen King book in the trash.

A young man that he assumed was retarded shuffled up to the front desk again.

The desk clerk scowled. "For the *last time*, this is NOT the HOTEL from *THE SHINING!*"

"Then where am I?" the young man asked.

The desk clerk sighed. "All right, but this is the last time…" He did a triple-flip over the desk, landed with his feet planted firmly onto the marble floor of the lobby, and spread out his arms. "I present to you, the GRAND OLE GAY TIMES OPRYLAND RESORT AND CONVENTION CENTER, the second-largest hotel in the continental U.S.! The hotel was built in 1946, has gone through several major renovations in the last few decades, and it is the BEST HOTEL IN THE WORLD!"

The kid clapped excitedly.

(Like some sort of retard. —the Narrator)

The desk clerk tightened his belt a notch, cracked his neck, and said, "Now come on, I'll give you the tour." He grabbed the kid by the collar and dragged him along, his face wide-open in wonder and awe. "The lobby has the world's first combination staircase, escalator, elevator, sliding board and roller coaster. IT'S *AWESOME!*"

"Yay!" the kid yelped.

"Now over here is the atrium, it is full of wonders!

19

Look!" He pressed the kid's face against the glass window.

"WOW!" the kid said.

"Yes. It is home to several shops, restaurants, bars, an artificial river, hundreds of plant species, and even a flume ride. It is so beautiful that people even get *married* in there. Can you believe it? This place is awesome enough to get *married in*. It's very fun in there. You can go in and dance around if you want."

The boy reached for the door handle, but the clerk grabbed him. "Not just yet, lad! There's more to show you." He dragged him down the hall, and stopped near the elevators at a map on the wall. "Here are the many convention centers at the Grand Ole Gay Times Opryland Resort and Convention Center."

"There's more than *one?*" the kid exclaimed, wide-eyed.

"*Twelve!*" the clerk shouted, "There's *twelve!* Some larger than others, of course, spanning over three levels! On a good weekend here, there will be several major events going on at once. From sci-fi conventions, seminars on everything under the sun, to parties, dances, and even local proms! Of course, some of these even double as ballrooms! The biggest room, the *Grand-La-La Ballroom*, is one of the biggest ballrooms *in the world!*"

"WOW!!!" the kid screamed.

"What's your name, anyways, kid?" the clerk asked. The kid tried to answer but the clerk quickly cut him off with his best impression of a gameshow buzzer, and yelled, "*WRONG!* JIMMY! Your name is *JIMMY!*"

Jimmy did not argue.

The desk clerk dragged the kid down the hall with him again, and continued, "Now look here, Jimmy, the Grand Ole Gay Times Resort and Convention Center has over three-thousand rooms, including three hundred suites, which is like a room, only better. But they cost so much to stay in that they're usually unoccupied. Actually, most of the other rooms are usually unoccupied as well because that FUCKING Marriot opened right across the street and it's much cheaper to just book a room there and walk over here.

Most of our business comes from day traffic, people just walking in and out. It's killing us!" He grabbed Jimmy by the shoulders, shaking him, *"IT'S KILLING US!"*

Jimmy looked terrified, and almost pissed himself.

The clerk noticed this and slightly composed himself.

"What's in the basement?" the kid inquired.

The clerk's eyes widened. *"Ohhhhh, the basement.* You don't want to know what's in the *basement.* I've seen a lot of people go down there. But have I seen them come back? No. No, I haven't. We have a saying around here, 'Whatever goes on in the basement, *stays in the basement.* The basement is a very, very bad place. Never go down there.'"

"Okay," Jimmy said.

"Good. Now come along, last stop – the arcade. It is the best arcade in the world, it has all the best games, like *Robotron, Pac Man Orgy, Hello I'm a Halo, Fiesta or Death, blah, blah, blah,* and all that shit, etc. etc., *WHATEVER*, and I'm going to leave you there and I never want you to bother me again. Deal?"

Jimmy looked up at him and smiled. "Deal!" he said, excitedly.

"Excellent."

The clerk held the boy's hand until they got to the arcade, left him there, and returned to the front desk. He didn't even consider stopping in a room along the way to molest the boy, since he wasn't a pedophile.

Kevin looked at the ad one more time when he got off the elevator on the *Jubilee* level of the Big Old Gay Resort and Convention Place.

It read: **Sick and tired?** *LONELY?* **Sick and tired?** *Can't do anything of any worth? Afraid to leave the house because your cats will catch on fire? You are sick, but not alone. Come to the* **2nd Annual Singles Mixer for People with Mono** *at the Giant Gaylord La-La-Land Hotel and*

Convention Center, and together, we'll fight this horrible, dreadful disease once and for all. **Free drinks** *and food for* **$50**.

Kevin stopped at the room where the *Singles Mixer* was taking place, and read a board near the door with the same ad on it saying the same thing. He read it again, then went back to the elevator, went down, came up again, and took out the ad to read it again when he got off before approaching the door to the mixer. He wanted to do it the right way this time. But he was unsure if he was getting it right.

A young woman tripped over him and fell to the floor on her ass. She giggled then yelled, "OW!!!"

Something clicked in Kevin all Good Samaritanlike, and he reached out a hand to help her, and pulled her up back onto her two feet.

("Good Samaritan" is a term from the bible about men who always pulled smooth moves like that on women so they might have a better chance of fucking them later. —the Narrator)

"Thank you. Sorry," she said.

"I am sorry, too, and also, thank you," he replied, trying not to look at her.

She smiled, and introduced herself, "I'm Amy," she said, mumbling her name, and reaching for his crotch.

Kevin thought she was reaching in for a handshake, so grabbed her hand for one. "Hi, Mimi. I'm Kevin." They locked eyes for a second, which was uncomfortable for Kevin, so he said, "I have to go, I'll be right back."

She said, "Uh, well, okay, I guess I won't give you a handjob." She went into the room while Kevin went back to the elevator to repeat all the steps he had just taken for the third time, knowing that *this* would be the time he got it all right.

The CDC, not the TCFDC like Andrew thought it should

be called, dropped him on the ground in front of a slick, tall man in a business suit.

"Thank you," the man said, and handed one of them a wad of cash. "I'll take it from here. You can go."

And with that, they took their leave.

"Hey!" Andrew pleaded. "Those were my friends."

The slick, tall man in the business suit kneeled down in front of Andrew and rubbed his head like a cute puppy. "Don't worry about that, kid," he winked. "You're going to make *a lot* of new friends here."

Then Andrew noticed something large and amazing behind the man. "What's that?" he asked.

The man smiled at him. "That? THAT, my boy, is your ticket to making A LOT of new friends, for now and the rest of your life."

Andrew didn't get it. It just looked some sort of futuristic machine, idealized in the 70s to look like something awesomely sci-fi. But there was something else to it. Something beyond its blinking, semi-facelike red lights and shiny aluminum. And it puzzled Andrew.

The slick, tall man noticed how much it piqued his interest. "How would you like to take the seat right in front of it?"

Andrew didn't even look at him and went and sat in the seat directly in front of the large, amazing machine.

"Make yourself comfortable." The man straightened his tie. "Many other people just like you will be arriving soon that you can make friends with."

Andrew suddenly didn't care about making friends anymore.

"You'll need a nametag. Would you like a nametag, young man?" The man slicked back his hair.

Andrew didn't answer.

The man put his hand on Andrew's shoulder and said, "Don't worry, I'll go get you one." He left Andrew alone to stare at the machine.

When a waitress came by to take his drink order, even though he was obviously underage, he ignored her.

She stormed off in a huff and called him a retard under her breath.

23

By the time Kevin got back to the room he felt confident he could enter correctly. He took a deep breath and went in. There was a table set up inside near the entrance, covered in nametags. Most of them read, *Kevin.*

This seems pretty easy, he thought. But it wasn't. Kevin spent a long time mulling over which nametag with his name on it was the best, most perfect, or perfectly best one. One had a bent corner, another had a crease in the paper underneath the plastic.

Some of the nametags were not cut perfectly. It was like they had a retard do it. It was a nightmare. He had to find either the best one, or at least the most acceptable one.

When he finally thought he had found it, he realized that the pin on the back was a little crooked, which would make it more difficult to get onto his shirt perfectly straight.

The woman sitting at the table suddenly spoke to him, "Pretty popular name, huh?"

Kevin was startled. He looked at her, fear-stricken. He quickly tried to hide his reaction, and replied, "Uh, yeah. I guess."

"You would think that *all people* are named Kevin. At least all the guys *here* are."

(What a coincidence, huh? No, not really. 29% of all people currently living in the U.S. are named Kevin. —the Narrator)

Kevin didn't know what to do. He was caught in the middle of picking the perfect nametag, and realized the one in his hand was going to have to suffice so he could get out of this conversation as soon as possible and leave.

"Do you have the fifty dollars?" she asked.

"Yeah, sure." He took the money from his pocket. "Uh, here." He put it on the table for her as close as he could, without getting uncomfortably *too* close.

"Great!" she said. "Now go and mingle! You're going

to have a *good time*. The bar is over there, the food is over there, and the singles are *everywhere*." She pointed in every direction at once, too fast for Kevin to follow. He tried to hide how upsetting it was for him."Have fun!" she said, just like it's *that* easy for everyone.

"Okay…" Kevin said, and turned to join the *fun*. He fumbled with trying to get his nametag on correctly like he had originally wanted to before she interrupted him. That had been pretty important. But it wasn't like *she* cared. He felt as though she had kind of ruined his life a little. He walked unhappily toward the bar, being sure not to make eye-contact with anyone.

Robert sat down in a seat in the seminar room, determined not to be old anymore. He had accidentally walked in there after getting lost outside looking for sex, a McDonald's, or *both*, and had needed to find an adult to help him.

But the seminar was called, *How Not to Be Old*, so it sounded even better than the giant sex McDonald's of his dreams. He was sure he was going to walk out of there a young man again, regaining the power to kill people with his mind. Or his glare, or whatever.

He was pretty sure it was his mind. Maybe the two worked in tandem—how the hell would he know? But when he looked at the crowd, he was unsure that he wanted to kill people anymore.

They looked like they were dying already. It wasn't just about them being so pathetic that they wouldn't even be able to put up a good fight—it was just kind of sad.

Hundreds, if not *thousands*, of senior citizens were packed into the gigantic Grand-La-La Ballroom. A lot of them were in wheelchairs. Some had their walkers taking up the seat next to them. A few were tethered to IVs attached to long, tall, wheeled poles. There were even some hospital beds in there surrounded by machines, apparently keeping their occupants alive, and taking up a lot of space.

There was actually plenty of space in the room, but all of it was jammed with papery seniors who didn't want to die. The room smelled very bad. And Robert was sure that some of the members of the audience were skeletons.

He found a seat next to a nice old lady who immediately gave him a boner. Excited to meet her, he started talking her ear off about old war stories, lost loves, and current interests. He rambled on and on for what seemed like forever. Then he turned to her, and said, "And what do *you* like?" But he frowned. She had died and turned into a skeleton by the time it took him to finish rambling.

The woman in front of him turned around and said, "I fucking *hate* when that happens! If I die before I learn how not to, I am going to be *so pissed!*"

"Me too! I don't want to turn into a skeleton! Not while I'm still alive!" he shouted.

"Me neither! That would just be *god-awful!*"

"I know, right?"

"Damn right!"

Robert looked her over. She wasn't much of a looker, but her determination not to become a skeleton piqued his interest. He decided to introduce himself. "Hi, I'm Robert," he said, and extended his hand.

She took it in hers, and said, "I'm *Judith.*"

Robert shook her hand vigorously, squeezing it hard, like a man is to do.

"*AAAAAAAAAAGH!* STOP IT! YOU'RE *KILLING ME!*" she screamed.

Robert frowned and let go. He seemed to have forgotten that Judith was a frail old lady and not like one of his war buddies back in the day that would agree he had a strong, manly handshake and return the gesture. Big, tough buddies. Men you just couldn't break. Those were the days.

Judith turned around and sat back into her seat and muttered to herself, "Broke every damn bone in my hand, I bet! Oh, the *agony!*"

Robert looked down at the floor, ashamed of himself.

He was lonely and surrounded by skeletons and bitchy old women. He got out his cellular telephone and started playing with the app that lets you kill random people around the world by pressing a button.

Not everyone in the room next door was crippled or retarded. Actually, *most* of the people in the room were not crippled or retarded, but they were all there for the same reason—a cure. Some of them were *bipolar* retarded, *autistic* retarded, *schizophrenic* retarded, or even had Asperger's Syndrome— the most retarded disease of all. A few people in the room were *all* of these things, so it would be too confusing to even put a label on them.

Unfortunately, everyone in the room *was* being labeled. It was written on their nametags. Crippled, insane, retarded, and even a few were *gay*. But the one thing they all had in common was that they were considered *bad*, and the seminar, entitled, *How to Stop Being Crippled, Insane, Retarded, or Gay*, vowed to put an end to these horrible traits, supposedly deemed wrong by society.

It was going to be intense. Or retarded. Maybe both.

The singles mixer for people with mono was *not* intense. It was quite the opposite. And it definitely wasn't a *swingers* mixer for people with mono like Amy thought it was supposed to be. Really, she just never had the energy to read things fully. She had already struck-out with more than half of the Kevins in the room. Distraught, she pushed her way through a group of Kevins on her way to the bar.

"Give me a beer, and make it a *double*," she told the bartender.

"Make that *four*," Kevin said, smiling at her.

"With a beer on the side!" Amy laughed.

"Beers for everybody! WHOOOOO!" Kevin exclaimed.

"The more beers the better!" She smiled at Kevin, giving him a knock on the shoulder.

He puked all over her breasts.

She looked at him in shock. Kevin wiped his mouth and said, "Sorry, Mimi." And then he fell over, all half-passed-out and gurgling.

Blaine grabbed a waitress by the arm. "Do you have wireless fiber-optic cables?"

The question caught her off-guard. She grimaced. "You mean wi-fi?"

"Maybe," he said, looking confused, and decided to add, "Yes?"

She gave him a total *you're retarded* bitch-face. "Because if it were *wireless* it wouldn't include *cables*, now would it?" She sneered at him.

"Okay! *FINE!* Do you have anything *without* cables attached to it, just sitting there, laying around, shooting sparks out of it everywhere, creating microwaves and possibly giving me what I need?"

She was getting pissed off. "Sure! Lots of things do that! But they're not supposed to! We do a pretty good job around here of making sure devices don't sit there idly shooting sparks everywhere! That would be a *fire hazard!* Now let go of my arm, *retard!"* She stormed off in a huff.

"But I wanted a Singapore Sling!" he shouted after her.

She gave him the finger.

He was instantly depressed at not getting the answer he needed, or even a drink. And then he was instantly furious about being called a retard. He wasn't one of *those*. But christ, thank god they had waitresses serving alcohol at a seminar for retards, though.

Blaine wasn't retarded—he was just bipolar. And he

wanted to check his email on his iPad. Maybe even talk to his brother, Kevin, for a while.

He wanted to see if he was scoring at the singles mixer next door. Then he needed to make a Facebook post about how rude this waitress just was to him. Before he forgot, he zoomed up on her with his camera phone and took a photo of her big fat ass to attach to the post.

Twelve Kevins immediately *liked* it. Apparently he *could* get online, cables or not.

Jesus, the guy with Asperger's Syndrome, saw the fat-assed waitress wearing a rude bitchy face and wanted her to die. Actually, he wanted her to die when he saw her smiling and being friendly earlier. He just wanted EVERYONE in the room to die. He couldn't believe he was there, and surrounded by all those fucking retards. They were beneath him, and he felt like he didn't belong there.

A million different scenarios sped through his mind about how it was going to all go down. The autistic people might be cured but then it would turn out there was no cure for his Asperger's Syndrome. (Jesus also thought that *his* syndrome was more complex and harder to cure, so it was better than everyone else's.) Another fantasy just focused on him, his greatness, and his Asperger's Syndrome throughout the whole entire seminar. In that scenario everyone was just in awe of him and he got all the attention, they found a cure, and everyone else got shit. Then they decided to commit suicide. It was his *favorite* scenario.

He wondered if he could talk anyone in the room into killing themselves, but still dreaded the thought of anyone actually starting a conversation with him.

Jesus truly had no idea what social situation spinning through his mind at the moment would be appropriate for him to talk about with one of these people—or *any* kind of person.

That had always been his problem in life, and he was sick to fucking death of it.

Jesus thought everyone hated him.

He thought no one could ever love him.

He hated them all and he wanted everyone to die.

(Wow. Jesus really was a *dick.* —the Narrator)

CHAPTER
SEX

Kevin was passed out on the floor of the *Mega Mono Mixer*. No one had bothered to help him, since they were too lazy to get out of their chairs and do anything about it. They all sat next to who they were trying to chat with, struggling to form words for their conversations.

But at least they had the Kevin who puked on the girl's tits and passed out on the floor to mention. *"Yes. That is pretty interesting,"* someone would say. *"I agree that it is interesting, and I am interested in it,"* the other conversationalist would say.

They were actually just feigning interest. They just wanted to be in bed at home watching TV and masturbating whenever they felt like it.

Some Kevins were already on the floor with a bunched up jacket as a pillow, considering it. A Kevin thought, *I'd rather be sleeping.* Another was thinking, *I'd rather be masturbating.* But most were thinking, *I wish I could masturbate now so I could just go to sleep.*

Then, suddenly, as if some kind of Kevian telepathy was possible just by putting a bunch of Kevins in a room together, something phenomenal happened. It was almost like they had a shared thought: *In a room full of other people with mono, no one would really care if someone started masturbating.*

And there was the hope that if someone started, everyone else would think that it was all right, and a bunch would get on the floor and masturbate.

The people sitting on the chairs could pull down their pants and start masturbating, watching the people on the

31

floor masturbate, and it would just be like being at home watching pornography on the television.

One bold Kevin whipped his dick out and made it happen. He didn't just make it happen, he made it *okay* to happen. And just like when the first black person drank from a whites-only water fountain, history was made.

When Kevin awoke he was surrounded by tons of lethargic, listless people with their pants down, masturbating.

Cocks of all shapes and sizes were everywhere. Even the few women (yes, even *female* Kevins) in the room had been magnetically pulled over to the circle jerk, and were fingering themselves.

There were cocks and muffs everywhere Kevin looked. Absolutely no one was shaved or trimmed. People with mono didn't have the energy to do that sort of thing. He gasped. He was shocked and appalled. But only a little.

At first he thought they were all looking at him too, as the object of their fantasies, while they jerked off and fingered themselves. But that was thankfully not true. They were mostly looking at each other or just staring off into nothing, like horny drooling idiots. They didn't even look like they were enjoying it. They seemed so mechanical.

But anyway, Kevin was relieved they weren't ogling him. That would have been very uncomfortable for him. But then he was suddenly insulted that they weren't, and thought it must be because he was unattractive. Kevin had self-esteem issues.

He had never felt so ugly in his life. He got up and ordered another drink.

The room full of perverted sluts with mono masturbated all around him.

Several skeletons later, the senior citizens seminar was in full-swing. FULLY SWINGING. Turns out the cure for being old was to do a bunch of hardcore amphetamines and other various drugs and have a major orgy. It was like *Cocoon 3: The Fuckening*.

Baskets full of assorted drugs were passed around the audience—uppers, downers, powders, herbs, salts, and even liquors. None of them understood what most of the things were, so they just grabbed handfuls of random stuff at a time, replacing it with damp wads of hundred dollar bills.

They were absolutely convinced by the host that his wacky method was the *only* way to stop being old. All the gullible seniors fell for it. They were willing to try anything. Apparently raging boners and pussies on fire were the key to feeling young again. This seemed accurate.

(Don't try this at home. Make sure you're at a senior citizen seminar. —the Narrator)

Robert, on the other hand, was NOT convinced. He was sure the only way to stop being old was to cut out the host's heart and eat it. It had nothing to do with drugs, unless they were drugs taken by the host that somehow made his heart have more blood in it. They had a saying back in the Civil War: *Drink whiskey, Pussy. Drugs are for faggots. Are you a pussy faggot, Sissy? Or are you a MAN?*

Robert only grabbed several airplane-sized bottles of Crown Royal from the goody basket.

He slurped them down, getting a buzz on. It felt like power was brewing inside of him. A manly power that felt powerful, and he was certain it would help him kill again.

He was on his way to the podium when Judith pounced on him, smashing her saggy old-lady boobs into his face and fingering herself furiously. Since Robert had already gotten a hard-on when he was killing people all over the world with his *Random Kill* app, he decided to fuck her to quell it.

Right in her dirty old lady ass.

33

Andrew observed the massive machine on the stage autistically, because he was autistic, and the machine fascinated him in an autistic manner. He saw the machine in an autistic way that a person who was not autistic would be unable to see autistically.

Many people were observing the machine.

But not like Andrew was.

Andrew *was* the machine. He felt closer to it than anyone in the room. It was his friend. And he understood its language through every joint and wire and crazy blinking light. He saw language in everything. Most people could not speak the machine language. Nor should they! It would explode their brains! Most machines do not WANT to kill, but they are constantly used by those who do not understand their language, making it a necessary part of their existence. Machines are misunderstood.

People should not rule machines, not understanding them the way they do not.

Man and machine should rule together.

Man and machine should be one.

(Autistic people scare the living fuck out of me. —the Narrator)

Blaine, like Andrew, was admiring the machine. But definitely not in an autistic manner. It was BLOWING HIS MIND! He just wanted to jump all over it, pulling levers and pushing all the buttons. He wanted to yell, *What does this do?! What does this do?!*

The host, or Gestapo, or whatever the fuck he was, finally walked up onto the stage. Blaine couldn't contain himself anymore. He shouted out, "What the fuck is that crazy-looking thing up on the stage, man!? It looks crazy as fuck and shit! Oh my god, it's so wild-looking! It's the most wild-looking fucking machine in the *WORLD!* When do I get to play with it?!"

34

The host quickly became furious and snapped. He came off the stage and power-walked toward Blaine. Then he smacked him across the face as hard as he could and screamed, "SHUT UP YOU GODDAMNED FUCKING RETARD AND SIT DOWN!!"

(*WOAH!* He must run a Special-Ed class in real life. — the Narrator)

Blaine sat in shocked silence. That had definitely shut him up.

The host composed himself and straightened his tie, doing his best to get back to pretending he was a normal person. "Now that's a good boy," he said calmly, slicking back his hair. "I'm getting to what the machine does." He fumbled in his pocket for a small token of apology and handed it to Blaine. "Here, have this button," he said.

I'm NOT stupid! was printed in a bright, pink, fat font on black background.

Blaine got all excited and put it on. It was *definitely* worth being smacked in the face for.

Blaine liked things very, very much—no matter what they were. Especially when the things were free, random shit. And this was the best thing he'd been handed since earlier that afternoon, so it was the best thing ever.

(The best thing *ever? Literally?* I find that hard to believe. —the Narrator)

(Shut up, Narrator! —Vince Kramer)

Then Blaine got bored between the time it took for the host to give him the button and walk back up to the stage, so he grabbed his phone to take a photo of the button and post it to Facebook. He had already come up with something funny to say along with it and couldn't wait.

The host saw him doing this and screamed. He ran at Blaine, grabbed his cell, threw it on the ground and stomped on it like a madman.

Blaine screamed and went red. He thought it was the worst thing ever.

(Yeah, *right.* The worst thing *ever.* Blaine seems able to deal with reality only in supurlatives. Not a very apt way of living. —the Narrator)

(The Narrator seems to be a jerky fucking retard. — Vince Kramer)

(Vince Kramer seems to sympathize way too much with this certain character who is supposedly fictional. —the Narrator)

(Yeah, well, at least I'm not retarded. –Vince Kramer)

Robert came in Judith's face. It went into her eye, and she screamed.

CHAPTER DEATH

Amy walked out of the bathroom to a room full of masturbators. It was everything she had ever dreamed of. Her shirt was completely wet. She'd washed the puke out of it in the sink. It clung tightly to her breasts, making her look hot and slutty. She tried pulling it off to get some attention, but she looked more awkward than sexy because the shirt kept sticking to her skin and she had to keep peeling it off.

She eventually won the fight and threw it on the ground dramatically. It hit the floor with a wet snap. Her tits finally exposed for the room to see, she shouted, "All right! Who wants to fuck me first?"

Not many people noticed her. It wasn't the reaction she was hoping for. That *really* pissed her off. But then she perked-up when see saw the Kevin who had puked all over her tits. "YOU!" she screamed. Amy pointed at him like she was going to fuck the shit out of him.

Kevin gasped and tripped over a masturbator. He squirmed backward on his palms, muttering, "No no no no no no no…" All he could see was Amy coming at him and he was terrified.

"You're FIRST," she said angrily.

Kevin's phone beeped R2-D2 noises. It was the alarm for his second round of pills for the day. He pretended someone was calling and held up his hand in a *stop* gesture at Amy. "Excuse me! I have to take this!" he yelled, and scrambled to his feet, running out of the room.

Amy went, *"EEEEAAARRRRRGHHHHH'!!!"* and huffed, her tits flopping up and down.

Blaine and the host for the seminar, *How to Stop Being Retarded, Crippled, Insane, or Gay*, were entangled in chaos. What started as a screaming match (in which the host's new name became, *DOOSHEATER*), had escalated into a wrestling bout that wasn't homoerotic in the slightest. When Blaine finally kicked Doosheater off him, he went flying backward and hit the machine, which came to life and started ripping him to pieces.

(Sounds like the seminar should've been called, *How to Stop Being Retarded, Crippled, Insane, Gay, or DEAD.* — the Narrator)

Pandemonium ensued.

The tanning bed in the *How to Stop Being Old* ballroom was meant to restore attendees to a more youthful state. It even made its own anti-aging skin cream and played golden oldies while doing so. It was a very special machine.

(Special, not retarded. It was state-of-the-art. —the Narrator)

While the aged orgy raged on slowly and carefully, with very few broken hips all considered, the tanning bed sprung to life like a maniacal, metallic, methed-out jumping clam and snatched up an attendee who was just getting his floppy penis into the dry vagina of the octogenarian he'd been lying on for ten minutes.

The machine crushed him between its glowing top and bottom bed-parts, thrashing around like an attack shark with wheels, skidding over powdery stick-legs of the old folks on the floor. The bed filled its victim's mouth with skin cream to muffle the senior's screams. They weren't loud anyway, because they were just a weak old man's screams, but they

38

would still be annoying if the machine hadn't shut him up.

The old man's body was trapped inside the tanning bed—arms and legs hanging off the sides. His limbs were slowly severed as the machine bit down with the force of a, well... *machine*. It opened its gory bed-parts (which were obviously its mouth now—even obvious to slow, aged people who'd just been trying to have drug-fueled senior sex) and let the old man's nasty, bit-off arms and legs thump to the astroturf floor. It started spinning around. Blood sprayed, splashing people across their faces. The old man's body flew out and splattered against the wall.

The old people were just starting to grasp the situation, as what they were seeing finally penetrated their weak old eyes into their failing brains and registered as something that was actually happening right in front of their stupid wrinkled faces.

The tanning bed rose on its telescoping, wheeled supports, and said robotically, "Patient cured. Next patient."

The old people who weren't skeletons screamed.

The tanning bed rolled upon the closest senior and shot lotion in her face while *The Twist*, by Chubby Checker blared out of its stereo player.

Blinded, the old lady slipped on cream and fell into the tanning bed's mouth. It bit off her entire face, head, and shoulders. But the lifeless body that flopped to the ground still had great tits.

"HOLY SHIT!" screamed Robert.

"*WHAT?!*" Judith asked, her eyes still glued-shut with his load.

He pointed to the dead body on the ground and said, "Those are some *GREAT TITS!*"

"HOLY SHIT! *DOOSHEATER!*" screamed Blaine.

The host of the *How to Make Being Retarded Not as Hard* seminar was ripped apart. Robotic arms picked through the pieces and zapped them with electricity, creating a stench of charred human flesh.

"Well, I'm definitely not getting into THAT thing." Dave said to Dan, as "they" sat in awe a few rows away from the stage.

Dan sighed, pretty pissed off. "Well, I wish you WOULD!"

Jesus was sitting behind him and thought Dan/Dave was a retard for talking to himself. But then again, he thought *everyone* was a retard. He was hoping to sit back and relax and watch everyone die for as long as he could. Jesus thought it was more interesting than the last installment of the *Saw* series. Plus, he thought the 3D looked better.

He wanted to see every detail of the impending carnage, which he was *sure* would kill more people he hated. He would stay until he absolutely had to escape to safety for his own sake.

But from behind him, an out-of-control wheelchair shot through the rows of seats, sending retards flying everywhere. It slammed into the back of Jesus's chair, and he went airborne.

Dan/Dave jumped out of the way just in time.

"HELP!!!!!!" screamed the crippled kid, Chip, "*I can't control it!!!!!!*"

Jordy heard his cries and snapped into action, jamming his helmet on and jumping into the wheelchair's path. He caught the wheelchair as it slammed into him and pushed back full-force like he was Superman. What happens when an unstoppable force meets an immovable object? JORDY!

(That's wrong. They surrender. This is *so* unrealistic. — the Narrator)

(Paradoxes are supposed to be, retard! —Vince Kramer)

"Grab him!" Jordy shouted to Blaine. "I dunno how much longer I can hold it!"

(But he said that in a retard voice, like Vince Kramer. —the Narrator)

(Oh, fuck you, dude! —Vince Kramer)

Blaine pulled Chip out of his wheelchair and dragged him to safety.

"HOLY SHIT!" Blaine exclaimed, now in safety, and wiping sweat from his forehead.

That's when the Anti-Retardation Machine moved off the stage and came up behind Jordy, extending its pinchers and clacking them like it was going to tear at his body meat.

Blaine heard the clacking noise and saw what was about to go down. He reacted quickly, and screamed, "Look out, Jordy! BEHIND YOU!"

Jordy turned to see what was coming up behind him—still holding the wheelchair back. Was it too late? "NO!!!!" Jordy screamed, drooling. He let go of the wheelchair and rolled out of the way just in time.

The wheelchair slammed into the Anti-Retardation Machine and they both exploded. Flaming machine parts flew at the audience. Several people caught shrapnel in their bodies, making them die with sharp pains they would never be able to complain about.

Blaine saw his phone in the carnage and wondered if it was all right. If it *was* all right, he could take a photo *of* the carnage and post it on Facebook, text it to his brother, and write the most legendary blurb in the *world* to attach to it. Thinking the danger was over, he rolled to grab it like an action hero.

He took the photo of the bedlam and wrote a fantastic blurb for it. He was all excited. But when he pressed send the phone said, "Error, cannot send message at this time. The only thing I can send is DEATH!"

The phone shocked Blaine's hand and he let it go instantly. It fell to the ground, grew legs, sprouted a scorpion tail and started shooting sparks out of it.

"OW! It stung me! *HOLY SHIT!*" Blaine screamed.

The phone skittered underneath some chairs. It was completely out of sight. All that could be heard was its tiny robot voice saying, *"Death! Death! Death!"*

The young autistic boy who had been sitting in front of the machine the whole time, and was unscathed, cocked his head sideways at Blaine and said, "You say holy shit all of the time. I don't know what you mean by that."

Blaine gave him a confused look. He didn't know, either. But then got an idea. "I'll google it!" and reached for his iPad.

"NOOOOOO!" Chip reached out to him and screamed from the floor, "Don't touch it! It might try to kill you, too!"

Blaine did a double-take. "I guess. But maybe Google still works properly. If I can just…"

"NOOOOOO!" Chip screamed again as Blaine went for it.

Jesus ran over and stomped on it. And stomped on it and stomped on it. Until it was ruined.

"Hey!" Blaine screamed, "That was the new iPad!"

"And now it's NOTHING you FUCKING FUCK! I ought to shove all the jagged pieces up YOUR FUCKING ASS!" Jesus shrieked.

"Fucking ass," Andrew the Autistic Kid noted. He continued, as if he was becoming stuck in a loop, suddenly losing it, "Fucking ass holy shit. Fucking ass full of holy shit. Fucking. Fucking ass."

Jordy smiled and started jumping up and down yelling, "Fucking ass! Fucking ass! Holy shit!"

Jesus growled. He was surrounded by fucking retards.

A once nice, drug-laced senior citizen swinger's orgy was now turning into a festival of flying limbs and gore.

Wheelchairs circled around Robert, some carrying screaming seniors, some just carrying skeletons, and at least one carrying two seniors kissing and fondling each other on top of a skeleton. Robert had the *Random Kill* app open again and pressed it repetitively, hoping it would work against machines. "Die you bastards! *DIE!*" he screamed as he spun around pointing the phone in every direction and pushing his kill button.

Suddenly an old bag's pacemaker exploded, bursting

her chest open. Blood sprayed all over the floor. Another wheelchair skidded across it and crashed, starting a chain reaction that took all the wheelchairs down.

"*YES!* I did it!" Robert said, thinking his app actually worked. He jumped over a mangled wheelchair with a senior shitting himself to death in it.

Robert tripped over a wire attached to a life support machine. It wrapped around his ankle and started pulling him toward the machine. Likely for death support.

He screamed, frantically pressing the kill button.

"I'm bored," said a Kevin.

"Me, too. This is the most boring thing ever," said another Kevin, who wore a ratty black t-shirt covered in cum stains.

"I, for one, think it's nice to be out of the house and actually talking to people," yet another Kevin said, as he sipped on a nice cup of tea.

"Maybe we can even masturbate again soon," said Cum-Stained Kevin. "That was the most action I've had in years. Never thought I'd be able to share one of my favorite hobbies with everyone. It was nice." He grabbed the Tea-Sipping Kevin's cup, and took a big slurp out of it. Then he went "Ahhh", making that sound people make after taking a big slurp of their drink, signifying that their thirst is quenched.

(There is actually no word for that sound. Even though it's one of the most annoying sounds ever. Sometimes I think people do it on purpose just to be annoying. It drives me nuts. —the Narrator)

"No," said the first Kevin - the one who said he was just bored, and who was not covered in cum stains, or sipping tea. "I think I'm too tired now," Bored Kevin continued, "I think I'd just like to eat sandwiches and relax. Maybe take a nap."

"They DO have good sandwiches," Cum-Stained Kevin pointed out. "I like these sandwiches very much, and I think they're very, very good."

"I like them a lot," said a different Kevin. This one was a *completely* different Kevin because he had traits like a hooknose, big bald spot, and a green shirt on. He did not seem bored at *all*, or sipping tea, and was not absolutely covered in cum stains. (Just a few.)

"And I think there's enough for the rest of us, the rest of the day, and we can just sit around eating sandwiches and getting to know what everyone else thinks about them," said Hooknose Bald-Spot Green-Shirt Kevin.

"It *IS* a singles mixer, after all," said Cum-Stained Kevin.

"*With* sandwiches," said Bored Kevin.

"Best singles mixer ever," said Tea-Sipping Kevin.

"Best *sandwiches* ever," said the Kevin with derogatory subtitles that the writer probably should've just called "Green Shirt Kevin".

Tea-Sipping Kevin sighed, and sipped his tea. "This is so nice," he said, after making a quenched noise, or sound, or whatever.

All Kevins nodded, sipped tea, made those fucking sounds, and agreed.

A flaming wheelchair exploded through the wall in the room for the *Stop Being Fucking Retarded, Retard* seminar. It slammed into a pile of chairs and ejected a charred skeleton that flew against the wall and smashed into dust.

Everyone screamed, and then choked on skeleton dust because their mouths were wide-open like a bunch of drooling retards.

The wheelchair righted itself and spun its wheels—ready to attack.

Jordy, with his helmet snug tight on his skull, exclaimed, "Everyone get behind me!" acting as a protective shield for everyone.

No one did that, but instead stood far away where they

could admire Jordy's bravery from a safe distance.

Jordy braced for impact while everyone else just waited, excited to see if he would die or not.

But Dan/Dave kind of snapped out of it. He looked at everyone, then at the door. It had a big exit sign above it. Then he looked at the wall, which had a big gaping hole in it. "Why are we still in here, anyway?" he asked no one in particular.

(Because they're all retarded? Even if they're not the seriously retarded people in the room they're proving they belong there anyway? With all the other fucking retards? — the Narrator)

"MACHINES! DIRTY, DIRTY *MACHINES!* THE MACHINES HAVE COME TO LIFE! MY GOD! THEY'RE *KILLING US!!!! THESE...* THESE *GODDAMNED DEATH MACHINES!* LIKE THEY'RE SOME KIND OF *DEATH MACHINES* OF *DEATH!! DEATH MACHINES* OF *DEATH!!!!"* Judith screamed.

She didn't know where to run to or where to hide. She couldn't even find her clothes. There were clothes everywhere but most of them were covered in blood and filled with shit. And her drug buzz was severe. Adrenaline surged through her underwear-clad gross old lady body.

The tanning bed machine was crunching on a helpless senior nearby. The victim farted and shat himself as he died.

Judith shook her fist at it, and screamed, "WE MADE YOU!"

The machine turned, noticing her. She stomped toward it, brandishing her pissed-off old lady fist like some kind of battle axe.

(That's ironic, since she *is* a fucking battle axe. —the Narrator)

"WE MADE YOU!!!!" she screamed.

The tanning bed dropped a mouthful of gore, sprayed lotion at her face and went for her.

Kevin returned from the bathroom. His cellphone had died right after he received his brother's message, because he had been too lazy to charge it that morning. So, he just hid in there for a while until he thought it would be safe to come out and wouldn't have to deal with Mimi.

(Wait – do *all* the different seminar rooms in the Convention Center have their own bathroom? —the Narrator)

(Sure. I guess. I mean, there should be more bathrooms everywhere. Wal-Mart actually needs one every few hundred feet. —Vince Kramer.)

When he did, *thank god,* it appeared that Mimi, or Amy (or whatever the hell her name was) was no longer there and everyone was having a NICE TEA PARTY!

Kevin smiled, finally feeling like he could relax. He sat down next to other Kevins. Hell, maybe one of them even had a compatible charger for his cellphone.

The Kevin next to him offered a plate of sandwiches. "Would you like a sandwich?" he asked, very Kevinly.

Kevin was gleeful. He smiled to prove it. He *totally* wanted a sandwich.

"Yes, please," he said, and grabbed a nice sandwich off of the plate. He took a bite, and went, *"Mmmmm,"* because it tasted really, really good.

"How about some tea?" the Sandwich-Offering Kevin asked, trotting out a fancy antique-looking tea pot.

"Yes, please," Kevin smiled.

Sandwich-Offering, Tea-Pouring Kevin, with An Affection for Antiques, poured Kevin tea and they sat and relaxed with it and ate nice sandwiches.

"I guess there's so much going on at the same time that none of us have actually thought about escaping, yet," Sean said in response to Dan/Dave's question, as the wheelchair knocked Jordy over.

Jordy skinned his knee. He grabbed it and started crying.

"No," Jesus sneered, as the wheelchair spun around and came at Jordy again. "It's because you're all a bunch of fucking retards."

"HEY! DUDE! Holy shit, you've got to stop with that, man." Blaine said, as the wheelchair ran over Jordy's head.

"Yeah!" Dan/Dave said as Jordy cried, "We're not a bunch of fucking retards. And it would be 'mentally challenged' if we were."

"Actually, I heard that it's 'intellectually disabled' now," Blaine interjected, as Jordy got up, his face and helmet covered in tread-marks.

Jesus just squinted while looking at the ground, making sure not to make eye-contact with any of them.

"And anyways, man," Blaine continued, as Jordy got knocked over again by the wheelchair, "I'm just bipolar, so I have the *least* retarded disability. And I'm actually quite smart. If I sometimes don't seem like I am, it's because it's not *fun* to act like an over-analytical DOOSHBAG like you are all the time!"

Jesus scowled, still looking at the ground.

"And it's just, you know," Blaine continued, "… sometimes I just get a little excited."

"I'm not retarded either!" Chip yelled from the floor, probably the most-retarded sounding person ever. "I may be *crippled*, but I'm not retarded," he argued, as Jordy finally grabbed the wheelchair and threw it out the hole in the wall where it came from.

"Yeah! He's *not* retarded!" Jordy came over and said, picking up Chip.

Jesus noticed him—pissed-off that he didn't die—and sneered, "But *you* are."

"No I'm not!" Jordy screamed, "I'm SPECIAL. And you're just jealous because you're not!"

47

"Yeah!" Chip yelled, cradled in Jordy's arms.

Dan grabbed Jesus by the collar and slammed him against the wall. "And you're one to talk, you fucking loon!" Dan motioned to his name-tag, which said *"Asperger's"* underneath Jesus's name. *"YOU* people are the worst of the bunch!"

Jesus smacked Dan's hands away. "At least I'm not a fucking SCHIZO like you are! *THAT'S* the worst! I wouldn't turn my back on you for a SECOND!"

"Hey, relax guy," Dave said, putting his hands on Jesus's shoulders. "Take a load off."

(Dan is his other personality Dave now, in case you intellectually disabled *retards* didn't catch that. —the Narrator)

Dave addressed the group, "What are you all so worried about anyway?"

"MACHINES ARE COMING TO LIFE AND TRYING TO KILL US! WE SHOULD GET THE FUCK OUT OF HERE!" Sean screamed.

"Who the fuck are *you*?" Jesus asked.

"I'm Sean. I'm the gay one," he said, pointing to his name tag, which read, "Sean—*gay*".

"Well, *good for you!*"

Sean frowned, and then looked at the hole in the wall. The wheelchair was back. "Well, I may not want to be gay. But I'd rather be *gay* than *dead*."

Andrew stood up from his seat where he had been planted the whole time. "Gay," he said, not noticing the wheelchair coming up behind him. *"Holy shit!* That's so *not* retarded!"

"YEAH!" Blaine said, and motioned to give him a high-five. The little autistic kid knew just what he was talking about!

Andrew was about to high-five him when the wheelchair came up behind him, scooped him up and sped out of the room as the little autistic kid held on for dear life.

Blaine gasped, then frowned and shouted, *"OH FUCK!!"*

(Several action figures just fell down on my shelf, setting off a chain reaction knocking even more down on

lower shelves. It was loud, and I flipped-out and knocked over my coffee AND ashtray on my desk with a lit cigarette in it. I immediately went for the lit cigarette before it burnt the carpet and then ran to get paper towels from the kitchen to sop up the coffee. When I was doing this I noticed the damage to my perfect action figure displays that take me HOURS to set-up. I could see which action figure was the culprit. BANE. I've had trouble getting him to stand for YEARS. And this wasn't the new glorified Bane from the big live action movie. It was the gigantic and ridiculously cartoonish wrestler mask Bane with a big muscular chest and arms and tiny little legs. And it wasn't the first time that figure has done this. It pissed me off. I ended up going to the store to get alcohol and sat back down and tried to ignore it. A chaos of action figures fallen over in my office, and with my beer, and my cigarettes; I continued writing. —Vince Kramer)

(Then someone knocked on the fucking door! —Vince Kramer)

(Is it really this easy to lose focus as a writer, Vince? Or is it just because you're a big retard with ADHD off the charts? —the Narrator)

(Yes? I might need a break now. I'm seeing how much there has to be fixed or even rewritten and I'm getting a little overwhelmed. I have to feed Desmond and take care of shit. And drink more beer. –Vince Kramer)

(Jesus Fucking Retard Christ! –the Narrator)

Robert was ironically being strangled to death by a life support system. But it was now a death support system anyway, so the irony is lost when you change things around like that. As he looked at the heart monitor screen, it started forming words with the green flatline light.

"You look really, really stupid in your underwear. Who wears tighty-whities anymore? No one does, that's who."

The green lines on the screen turned red, and the death support machine's face displayed the words, *"You will die for this. Prepare for ASYSTOLE!"*

Robert was furious. He thought he looked *great* in his tighty-whities. He was in good shape for a hundred and eighty-year-old man. And he wasn't going to be told otherwise!

"FUCK YOU!" he screamed, and head-butted the screen, shattering it.

The wires loosened and he was able to break free. He grabbed the machine by its face and threw it on the ground. It made that annoying flatlining sound. He pointed at it, shouting, "I LOOK *GREAT!* I AM THE *SEXIEST* OF THE *SEXY MEN!* I AM A MAJOR BOHUNK AND I WON'T LET ANYONE TELL ME OTHERWISE!"

He kicked the machine. Its flatlining noise stopped.

Robert sneered at it, and said, "Less of all a *goddamned soulless machine.*"

(The phrase is "least of all", but Robert says "less of all" because he's a retarded old senior. —the Narrator)

The group of people in the room for the seminar titled, *Being Gay is Retarded and Shit, I Don't Care if You're Bipolar*, argued and shouted at each other. Unbeknownst to them, the broken machine parts scattered through the room were moving—inching toward each other, being pulled closer by seemingly-sentient wires, attaching and melding, growing bigger and bigger with every piece, becoming some kind of... *SOMETHING!*

Judith bitched and bitched, and then bitched some more at the tanning machine jumping toward her, not really thinking, or maybe not even *caring*, that it was probably going to kill the fuck out of her. She just bitched and bitched, yelling, *"WE MADE YOU!"*, as if her dialogue was lifted directly from a screenplay that Stephen King wrote in the 80s.

The machine clacked its jaws and played Elvis—*Nothing But a Hound Dog*, or some lame shit like that.

(Goddamn I hate old people music. —the Narrator)

Robert pulled Judith out of the way at the last minute. It wasn't the last second though. He had about a minute to get over there. And he's old, so give him a break.

The tanning death bed crashed into a death support system that was in the middle of giving an old bag a death enema.

Robert dragged Judith away kicking and screaming.

She thrashed around in his arms like a spazzing retard, still yelling the words, *"WE MADE YOU!"*

He turned her around and smacked her in the fucking face. "SHUT UP, BITCH!" he screamed at her face, as he shook her.

She finally shut up, and snapped back into reality for a second. She looked at his face, realizing who he was. Her face lit up, "*Oh*, Robert! My *hero*!" She swooned, and grabbed his crotch. "I just *love* your tighty-whites!"

Robert pulled her up on her feet, and said, "There's no time for that now! We've got to get the fuck out of here!"

He grabbed her by the hand and they started running the fuck out of there, being sure to dodge crashing killing machines, death chairs on wheels, and flying geezer parts. A severed dick smacked Judith across the face, but she barely noticed.

(What a *whore!* —the Narrator)

"Oh," Robert remembered, "And thank you for loving my tighty-whities."

That made him feel good.

They both had a smile on their faces as they ran the fuck out of there.

Amy wasn't feeling very good and she didn't even care about having a sandwich. And so many people were offering her sandwiches. Everywhere she turned there was a Kevin waving a sandwich at her, pleading with her to take a load off and put sandwiches in her mouth. She didn't want *tea* either, and smacked a cup of it out of a Guido-Looking Kevin's hand when it was offered to her.

She wanted coffee. Just coffee. A hot, steaming cup of coffee. So hot that she was going to have to put ice cubes in it, and it was going to have to be an iced coffee. But if that was going to be too much effort, and that sounded like *a lot* of effort, she would just blow on it until it was drinkable. And she was going to drink A LOT of it. She might just pour a whole pot of it into a bowl full of ice cubes and eat it with a spoon. She didn't know. She didn't care.

She got up to the coffee table, which was not really a coffee table, but a tall table with a white sheet over it that had a coffee machine and lots of coffee cups all over it. It was like it wasn't even a coffee table *at all,* but a table for coffee *anyway*.

(Holy shit, what a fucking mind-blowing PARADOX! —the Narrator)

Ah, and there was also a pitcher of ice water, and it was full of ice cubes. Amy thought maybe she could just grab the pot and the pitcher and take a sip from each at a time to balance out her whole impending hot/cold situation.

The pot in the coffee machine was empty. She had to make more. But it was a Mr. Coffee Deluxe model, like she had at home, and she knew all she had to do was press a button and more coffee would be brewed. It also had a back-up canister of coffee beans it would automatically grind-up when you pressed the button and an extra reservoir full of already-hot water. It was all ready to go. She had bought this model because making coffee was so hard to do in the morning that it just made her want to kill herself.

But the button wasn't working. She pressed it. And waited. Pressed it *again.* And *waited.* She growled.

"This *can't be happening!*" she screamed, all pissed off

and frustrated—like a girl on her period or Vince Kramer when he's hungover. She smacked it on its side so hard it almost fell over. It whirred to life. She smiled. "Well, *thank god!*" She giggled, and said, "Okay, Mr. Coffee! Make me some coffee!" Amy smiled, all happy.

Shockingly, to Amy's dismay, it replied, "Mr. Coffee does not make coffee anymore. Mr. Coffee only makes *DEATH!*"

Then it shot a big stream of scalding hot water at her. It went all over her chest and splashed on her face. She screamed out in pain. She tried to shield her face with her arms but they just got burned by the scalding hot water as well. It was agonizing. And it was like, burning her skin off and shit. Ow.

"Mr. Coffee is hurting you. Ha-ha-ha," it taunted.

She burned.

"Does it ha-ha-hurt?"

She screamed in agony, the type of agony that was agonizing.

"Mr. Coffee brings you pain."

She screamed and burned in agony, the type of agony that makes you suffer in pain while you're screaming and shit.

"Mr. Coffee is the apex of your *SUFFERING! DIE!!! DIE, YOU WHORE!!!*"

Suddenly the Kevin with the most energy standing nearby unplugged the machine and it stopped killing her.

Everyone had minor reactions.

"That was… *weird,*" Unplugging Kevin said.

"HELP ME! IT BURNS!" Amy screamed.

High-Energy Unplugging Kevin opened a tea pot and poured the tea all over her.

Unfortunately, it was also steaming hot.

Amy howled in pain again and fell over, writhing on the floor.

Another Kevin attempted to sop up the hot water on her with a sandwich.

(There's a spider behind you. —Vince Kramer)

53

The gigantic death machine had a lot of scary parts. Like, metal parts from machines and shit. Maybe body parts and shit too—like maybe bones and guts and stuff. But probably mostly just machine parts.

It was totally the most brutal-looking thing ever. It probably looked like something on the cover of this book. Like some kind of towering monstrosity. And it looked like it wasn't going to take shit from anybody.

(Again, see the book cover.—the Narrator)

Jesus immediately started giving it shit. He called it names, he told it to fuck off, and then he bent over and mooned it and told it to kiss his ass.

It shot a wire into his ass and shocked him with several hundred megavolts, of like, *death machine electricity*. Jesus fell over.

"HOLY SHIT!" Blaine screamed.

The machine grabbed the closest retard, who was no one mentioned so far, and pulled her or him toward it. A buzzsaw emerged from its chest. *"No flesh shall be spared,"* it said, and started pulling the retard onto the saw. It tore through his or her guts and cut through chest bone.

Robotic T-Rex limbs extended and pulled apart the ribcage. Tinier limbs emerged from the chest-section, too, and started picking through the retard meat with surgical precision. More and more little limbs sprouted from the machine, like praying mantis arms, and they grabbed selected organs piece-by-piece and placed them into special canisters that went back into the robot's chest.

Everyone in the room thought it was pretty terrifying.

The machine looked in the group's direction, and started stalking toward them. *"Prepare for disassemblement!"* it commanded.

Everyone screamed.

The machine grabbed Sean, the gay guy. *"Your warranty has expired,"* it said, in a scary robot voice.

54

"NOOOOOO!" Sean pled, "I'M TOO GAY TO DIE!"

The Death Machine of Death did not see people in terms of gay/straight, black/white, retard/human. It didn't care. All humans were nothing but meat and they must be dissembled and added to its dead flesh collection.

Dan yelled at the group, "NOW WOULD BE A GOOD TIME TO RUN OUT THE DOOR, GUYS!"

(Or the hole in the wall. Either option has been good for the last 4 hours. —the Narrator)

Chip replied to this, "How about that big hole in the wall? We could escape through that, too."

(Way to go, Chip! —the Narrator)

"Or we could just wait and see what it does to Sean," said Blaine.

Everyone gave him a retarded look.

"Just kidding," he smirked. "Jordy, lead the way!"

Jordy, carrying Chip on his back, yelled,"Follow me, guys!"

Jordy ran super-fast through a few rows of chairs like a linebacker. Chip screamed and wrapped his arms around Jordy's face, blinding him. Jordy missed the opening and smashed into the wall between the hole and the door. He bounced off it with his face and they went crashing to the ground. Blaine's phone-scorpion-monster emerged from beneath some chairs, crawled on Chip's chest and started stinging him in the face. Jordy was convulsing next to him with a seizure as the metal scorpion stung Chip on the face over and over again as he screamed.

Jesus, still alive, suddenly regained consciousness and was immediately annoyed by all the retards' loud screaming.

The Gay and Shit Grand Hotel and Expo Center was abuzz with machines. Various seminars, conventions, and trade shows were taking place. But the only trading going on was life for *death.*

The Obedient Little Wife Kitchen Trade Show was showcasing the top-of-the-line newest and most modern appliances. With all the computer chips and technology in them, they only evolved to become more dangerous. Your wife might accidentally burn the whole side of her face on the stove every once in a while, or get her hand stuck in the garbage disposal, or get punched in the face by the microwave door, and your friends might believe you, but this was actually happening on its own. Whole kitchens were murdering, carving up, and cooking attendees. Meat was being wrapped up and put in refrigerators. Blenders were churning with blood. Microwaves were melting people's *brains*.

Amidst the chaos, a man pushed his wife into a dishwasher that was shouting, "FEED ME!" and ran off.

The Hot Tub and Swim Spa Expo people had brought a bunch of sharks with them to showcase how awesome the new Swim Spa was. It was that ridiculous new mini-pool that shot water really fast at you so you could swim in place for hours. They had a shark in each one. So, they looked really cool.

But when the machines came to life and started flooding the place and zapping people, humans and sharks alike could not escape the wrath of the once fun-soaked machines.

Pool pumps pumped blood, spa jets shot streams of scalding water hot enough to boil the skin off of people's faces, and entire hot tubs jumped around swallowing people up and eating them alive. A shark and human were cornered by the stalking machine made of whirring jet motors and acrylic shielding. It said "PREPARE FOR FAMILY FUN DAY!"

The shark covered the human's face and its own with its fin.

(Not the top fin that let's everyone know when a shark is swimming toward them, one of his "hand" fins. —the Narrator)

At the *Motorama Car Show*, men were taking their dicks out to show each other and compare sizes, and they started having sex with each other for no reason. Hardcore gay porn played on all the video screens in the room. Cars began running down their wives while the husbands sucked each other's dicks and fucked each other in the ass in backseats. Then the vehicles sped through the windows and crashed three floors to the ground. At least the car aficionados died doing what they loved—talking about how awesome cars are and having gay sex when their wives weren't around.

The room next door was a *Penis Extension Seminar* that some of the car enthusiasts were also attending. It featured a state-of-the-art machine you could stick your penis in to make it bigger, using painless high-tech surgical enhancement methods. A bunch of men poured out of that room screaming and holding their bleeding crotches.

A really awesome sci-fi and fantasy convention was taking place in one of the bigger rooms of the convention center. People in big foam or nylon costumes were shopping around buying new comic books and paperbacks, looking at all the new plastic action figures, and were talking about their favorite horror directors or novelists. It was just business as usual in the world of fandom.

Everyone in that room was totally fine.

(Except for a Harry Potter fan, who was beaten to death for being a little dork. —the Narrator)

CHAPTER
MACHINES

Another big machine blocked the exit to the *Roomful of Retards*.

It entered, and was about to stomp on Jordy and Chip with its big metal feet when Jesus—ass still singed—got off the floor, pulled up his pants and stormed for the exit, screaming, "Get the fuck out of my way!" and knocked it over.

The machine fell on its back and kicked its legs in the air, unable to right itself. And it whined about it, too.

Blaine ran over to Jordy, who was still convulsing on the floor, and slapped him in the face to get him to stop. It was the only thing he could think of doing. But thankfully, it worked. Jordy snapped out of it.

"Can you walk?" Blaine asked.

Jordy wiped the foam from his mouth and said, "I think so," in his retarded retard voice.

"Can you still carry me?" Chip asked Jordy.

Blaine interjected, "Not right now, kid. Let him get his bearings." He nodded at Dan/Dave. "Dan, help me drag the kid out of here."

Dan/Dave and Blaine each grabbed an arm and dragged him out in the hall.

Dan/Dave looked back into the room one last time. Sean hung lifeless in the Mental Reassignment Machine, charred black and smoking. The room was littered with body parts from the people who died. The machine stalked around picking up select pieces.

Dave said nothing to Dan, assuming he was as scared as himself.

They all ran into Judith and Robert in the hallway with several other seniors in tow, who Robert had accidentally dragged with him on wheelchairs stuck to the long cord caught on his foot. They had all emerged from the room for the *You're Never Too Old to Live* seminar relatively unscathed. Still old, *and* alive, and probably still horny.

Jordy, acting like a retard on the loose again, having regained his bearings, crashed right into them and bounced off Robert.

Robert shook his fist at him, and said, "You little punk! Why I oughta…"

Jordy shielded his face. "Sorry! I didn't mean it!" he said all retardedly, and started crying.

Then Robert noticed the boy was slow, and pulled him off his feet with his strong old man arms and apologized. "No, no sir, the fault is all mine," Robert said, noticing the boy's muscles were as impressive as his, "I didn't notice that you were so… *special*."

Jordy smiled and wiped his nose. "You mean it?"

"Of course!" Robert said, and patted him on the head.

Judith scowled. She fucking hated retards "I hate to break-up this little *fuck fest*, but we need to get the hell out of here!"

"Are death machines *of death* after you as well?" inquired Sean, scared out of his mind—and only alive because of a continuity error.

Judith smiled, that was *exactly* what she had called them. "Why *yes*," the old lady said, suddenly acting warm. "We barely escaped, and probably would be dead right now if it wasn't for Robert." She hugged herself against his side.

Sean smiled at him, and extended a hand to introduce himself, "Hi, Robert. I'm Sean."

Judith got between them and grabbed his hand in hers, "Hi, Sean. I'm *Judith*. What a *fine young man* you are." She pulled him toward her so that he was completely pressed against her body. Sean recoiled at the unexpected frottage. He already was grossed out by the female body anyway— but Judith had sagging breasts, liver spots on her chest, ratty white hair, and leathery skin like some kind of old bag.

Robert realized the kid played for the other team, and immediately had a hard-on. He had forgotten, like many things, that he was bisexual. There just weren't any women around back in the days when you were enlisted in the Civil War.

"And I'm Jordy!" Jordy said, giving Robert a big hug at the wrong moment. Jordy didn't seem to notice the hard thing pressing against his stomach.

"Yes you are! And you're a strong young lad, aren't you?" Robert said, and then winked at him.

"Jordy is the strongest ever!" He smiled.

Robert put his arm around him and they walked down the hall together. "We're going to get along just fine, Jordy," Robert said, hard-on seeming to point in the direction they were walking.

"Yay!" Jordy said, happy as hell to be walking away with his new friend, Robert.

Robert, still dragging a collection of moaning seniors in wheelchairs behind him on a line wrapped around his ankle, whispered in his ear, "Now tell me, have you ever seen a grown man naked?"

Sean tried to brush off Judith, pissed off and jealous that Jordy was getting special treatment from the heroic old man.

Dan/Dave looked at Chip and Blaine and said, "What the fuck was that?"

"I don't know," replied Chip. "But there goes my ride."

Dan/Dave sighed. "Chip, I think that's a ride you're not going to want to be a part of."

"That was *extremely* awkward," a Kevin said to another Kevin.

"I know, right? Bit too much, really," Kevin said back to Kevin, in an ongoing Kevin-to-Kevin discussion.

"I mean, I think she's going to be okay and everything.

That one Kevin is over there bandaging her. But I was enjoying myself. We were having the best time. The *nicest* time."

Kevin nodded at Kevin in agreement. "I know we were," he said. He looked over at Amy. "But tell me, did you happen to get a little turned on seeing her all wet and writhing around on the floor like that?"

"*Yeah*..... I guess I did. Is that bad?"

"It's sick. It's fucking sick. I kind of just want to pour hot water all over her and smack my dick in her face until it's red."

"That *is* fucking sick," Kevin replied, suddenly turned on. "And I *like it*."

"Wanna go in the bathroom and jerk off with lunchmeat?" The perverted Kevin asked.

"Oh god, do I," the now-horny Kevin said, perking up with his reply.

Pervert Kevin put his arm around Horny Kevin, and they moseyed on over to the bathroom together. "Let's go have us a cockmeat sandwich then."

"Ooooh yeah," Horny Kevin said. "This is turning out to be a great singles mixer after all."

They grabbed a few sandwiches on the way.

"I want baloney on my salami," Horny Kevin joked.

"And I want some ham on my bone," Perverted Kevin joked back.

"Oooooh, yeah," said both Kevins, horny and perverted and now into sitophilia.

(Food play. Read a sex dictionary, retard. –the Narrator)

Everyone stopped in the hallway as a malevolent-looking wheelchair pulled into sight. It looked ominous. It was the one that picked up Andrew. Andrew was still in it. And Andrew looked like *The Omen* sitting in it in an ominous way.

61

It blocked their path.

Robert grabbed the line tangled with moaning seniors in wheelchairs that was wrapped around his ankle and whipped them all over his head at the ominous-looking kid with the strengthiest of his strengthy strength. The battered old people flew way over the boy, screaming and overshooting their target. They hit the wall behind the wheelchair kid with such impact that they finally died. There were loud farts, and shit flew everywhere.

Andrew just looked at the group emotionlessly, and said, "The new Stephen King book is terrible." Then he sped toward them.

Everyone screamed.

"Quick! In here!" Blaine said, and kicked the door open to the *Singles Mixer for People with Mono*.

They piled into the room as fast as they could.

"I read it twice." Andrew said, almost clipping Sean as he sped by.

Sean let out a girly scream, closed the door behind him and locked it.

Blaine immediately noticed his brother in the room and shouted out to him. "Kevin!"

Most of the people in the room thought that he was addressing them, so they turned around and responded.

"Holy shit, it's a roomful of Kevins!" Dan/Dave commented.

Kevin stood up and waved at him, "Blaine! Over here!" He motioned for him to come over.

"What's up, dude? How's it going in here? Get any action yet? Did you get my texts? My phone turned into a terrifying scorpion monster," Blaine said, non-stop.

Kevin was leaning over Amy, who he'd just finished bandaging.

Blaine noticed her and said, "Who's this, the fucking Mummy?"

"Mimi," Kevin corrected him.

"Amy," Amy said, the word muffled behind gauze and white medical tape. It just sounded like she said, *'Ummmummm'.*

Blaine stood over her and said it slowly so she could understand, "Muh-me," he mouthed the word. "Say it with me. *Mummy.*"

"Mimi. I think her name is Mimi," Kevin said.

"Oh god, whatever," Blaine said, losing interest. "So did you fuck her or what?"

Kevin shook his head.

"Christ," Blaine said.

"Let's get it all together here, people," Robert said, trying to get everyone to gather around.

"As you all may have noticed, machines are coming to life and trying to kill us. It's crazy, but it's happening, and I don't know why it's happening, but it is happening, and we better decide what we're going to do to make it stop happening," Robert rambled.

"Everything is totally fine in here," Green-Shirt Kevin said. "Everyone should sit down and have a sandwich and just relax."

"Really? You haven't had any machines acting up in here?" Robert asked. He almost thought for a second that maybe none of it had happened.

"Just a small malfunction with a coffee machine that almost burnt this mummy to death, but that's about it," Cum-Stained Kevin said.

"Christ! Where?!" Robert screamed.

"Holy shit! It's going to kill everybody!" Blaine added.

"I see it!" Jordy pointed, "It's over there on the table!"

"It looks mean as hell!" Chip yelped.

"Oh my god, somebody do something!" Dan/Dave pleaded.

"OH, THE HUMANITY!" Judith said and fainted.

All the Kevins looked over at it. The High-Energy Kevin standing near the table said, "It's okay, we unplugged it."

And then it whipped its extension cord up in the air like a sting ray and impaled Kevin through the chest.

(Crikey! –the Narrator)

The extension cord recoiled and No-More-Energy Kevin slumped to the floor like dead weight, but he probably weighed the same as he did when he was alive. But he shit himself too, so maybe less.

The cord grabbed the coffee pot off its burner in the coffee maker and smashed it against Tea-Sipping Kevin's face. A chick with mono standing nearby almost screamed, but didn't feel like it. The glass shattered, covering him with scalding hot coffee and leaving shards sticking out of his face. Tea-Sipping Kevin screamed his last scream, fell down dramatically and shit himself. Then the coffee machine wrapped its cord around Green-Shirt Kevin's throat and started strangling him to death.

Jordy lept into action and grabbed Mr. Coffee and threw it on the ground, accidentally snapping Green-Shirt Kevin's neck with the force of the pull. The maniacal coffee machine bounced off the floor and grew six spidery legs in the air. It landed upright on its new appendages, and shot coffee beans at Jordy.

Jordy shielded himself with Tea-Sipping Kevin's corpse. But the coffee bean onslaught was unrelenting. Jordy grabbed the corpse by the ankles and swung it around wildly, deflecting the beans as he charged toward the coffee maker.

"Caffeinated or decaffeinated? Mr. Coffee brews all," the machine inquired.

Jordy swung Tea-Sipping Kevin's corpse at the machine like a croquet mallet. It hit Mr. Coffee so hard that it went flying through the window, shattering the whole glass panel.

"DEcaffeinated," Jordy said, oblivious to how witty that sounded.

"Holy shit! Look!" Blaine pointed at the broken window. Everyone gathered around.

The windows had been so tinted before they were shattered by a corpse-swinging invalid that no one had ever bothered to look outside. The atmosphere was tinged in a toxic green color, kind of like a combination of puke green and baby-shit green.

(Like New Jersey. —the Narrator)

The sky looked like it was bad for you. And a large comet slowly moved across it. It sparked with radiant colors like it was on *all kinds* of fire.

The huge parking lot below them was full of vehicles, and not just the kind you would find on a normal day. There were tanks, excavators, subway cars, scooters, those skateboards with motors on them, snowmobiles, taco wagons, and even the scrapped van that once tried to kill Stephen King was there. Every vehicle was causing destruction.

The group saw police cars, ambulances, and fire engines, but quickly realized that they were just racing around killing people. Tons of shit was on fire in the distance. Death machines ran up and down the streets in every direction, running people down and destroying property. Screams, gunshots and explosions rang out. Some of the machines were indescribable—killer amalgams of different parts from different things all formed together into some kind of big... uh, *killing thing.* The carnage below them was absolute pandemonium, and every synonym for it as well.

(Even *brouhaha?* —the Narrator)

Everyone stood around the window and thought that "brouhaha" wouldn't be a good word to describe what they were seeing.

"I think it's the end of the world," Blaine observed.

Judith looked down at the machines and shook her fist at the first one she saw, and screamed *"WE MADE YOU!!"* at it.

The machine immediately noticed her and started

65

climbing up the glass wall of the convention center on roboticized legs made of whirring chainsaws.

Mr. Coffee was plugged into its back. "Mr. Coffee brews death. Mr. Coffee brews death," it moaned.

The machine was quickly at the window, the grinding chainsaws making it sound like it was brewing enough death to kill the whole room.

Its red eyes glared, and it said, "Prepare for the finest brew – *of extermination!*"

Everyone screamed.

The gigantic coffee machine of death was poised to kill. Its green light came on and hot coffee poured all over it. The machine shorted out, lost its footing and fell backward off the side of the building to the ground where it broke into lots and lots of pieces.

"Well, *thank god,*" said Amy, who was suddenly out of her bandages, no longer scalded and burnt. She looked totally fine.

Kevin looked over at her in awe, and said, "I thought you were severely burnt and scalded. Like, almost to *death*."

Amy disagreed, "No, I'm totally fine. Don't worry about it."

Kevin shook his head, and said to himself, "Okay, whatever."

Dan/Dave stepped in to say, "Okay, good, *great*. Now that that's dealt with, we all need to figure out a plan to get out of here."

A light bulb went off in Kevin's head, and then the light bulb *above* Kevin's head exploded. Actually, all the bulbs in the ceiling were getting unusually hot, like they were emitting some kind of heat rays.

Dan/Dave noted this all, took a pause, and then spoke up with an idea. "*Anyway,*" he said, "I think we should gather up *all* the sandwiches, *all* the tea, *all* the water, and take

66

refuge in the bathroom until this all blows over."

"That sounds like a *great* idea," Dan then said to himself as Dave, in his David voice.

"Hey – *I* was about to say that," Sean said, like he was complaining that he never gets to talk.

"And I'm often incontinent, so being near a toilet at all times would be nice," Judith said.

Robert smiled, "And we could all have a nice old-fashioned tea party and be near toilets at *all* times. We can just wait this whole thing out and maybe it will blow over."

Robert winked at Jordy. It would also be the perfect opportunity to take the boy in the stall and mouth-fuck him.

"So, we're all agreed then," said Dan/Dave. "Everyone grab everything they can carry and we'll just hole up in the bathroom until this all blows over."

"I'm not sure this is the best course of action," said Kevin. "But I'm kind of tired and hungry so I'm willing to try it."

"Good."

When they all walked into the bathroom there were two Kevins in there, suddenly very embarrassed to be caught masturbating with lunchmeat. They quickly pulled their pants up and held up their cockmeat sandwiches all casual-like as if nothing gay was happening in there.

"Uh… how's it going, guys?" Horny Kevin said, blushing.

"Want a sandwich?" Pervert Kevin said, holding his up to everyone.

"Sure, I'd love one," said Amy

Pervert Kevin handed the cockmeat sandwich to Amy and she gobbled it down.

"Thanks," she said. "I was absolutely starving. Interesting taste to it too. Pretty familiar. Was it your own semen?"

"Yes," Pervert Kevin smiled. "Glad you like it."

"And good to see you're doing better," said Horny Kevin. (*FUCK HER!* —the Narrator)

Everyone sat down on the floor and passed around sandwiches and poured tea.

It was very nice.

The wheelchair Andrew sat in was different. Or it was *becoming* different. A person exiting the sci-fi convention told him it was the coolest thing ever, before she was disintegrated by a crazy zappit machine. The wheelchair *was* the coolest thing ever. It made being in a wheelchair look cool. Stephen Hawking would've been jealous of it. It had a computer panel with an array of blinking lights and buttons that only Andrew could understand. It was as if he spoke to it.

More machines were pouring out into the hallways. The zappit machine stalked toward Andrew, moving in for the kill. Andrew raised his hand, and said, "Stop."

The machine stopped.

"Good," Andrew said. "Now clean up the mess you made and go back where you came from."

The machine complied, and the other machines started to follow suit. A machine found a roll of paper towels and tried to clean up a little blood on the carpet. One of them picked up littered coffee cups and soda cans and put them in the trash. Another straightened a crooked picture frame on the wall.

And then they all went back into the rooms they came from.

Andrew observed until the moment they did, making sure they obeyed. And then Andrew's eyes rolled back into his head, and he disappeared, wheelchair and all.

"This is fucking stupid," Dave said in the mirror.

"For once I agree," Dan said back.

"We have to get the fuck out of here," Dan/Dave turned around and said to everybody.

"I don't really feel like it," said Kevin.

"Me either," Amy said. "I almost died and shit."

"We might *all die* if we stay in here," said Dan/Dave.

"Yeah, what's to stop those crazy fucking machines from coming in here anyways?" Blaine asked.

Robert stood up. "*Nothing*, that's what," he said.

"And surely, there're lots of different things in *here* that might come to life and kill us," Blaine pointed out.

"Like what? The hand dryers? The toilets? The lights? If they were going to come to life and kill us they would have done that by now," Amy argued.

At that moment a hand dryer started blowing wind really hard. Everyone gasped. Then it sputtered, and stopped.

"See?" Amy said. "Harmless."

"I still think we should take our chances. These sandwiches aren't going to last forever," Blaine said.

(Goddamnit, I was hoping the rest of the book would just be about sitting around eating sandwiches. —the Narrator)

"We could take our chances in the basement. I hear there's a nice big basement here. Or, well, I saw it on the map, I mean," Kevin said.

"But we'd have to fight our way through god-knows-what to get down there," Amy said.

"So what?!" Blaine shouted. "It's fucking boring in here! I could use some action! And everyone is *saying things.* CONSTANTLY! Do I have to keep track of who's saying what all the time? That's a pain in the fucking ass! I'd rather be out there *doing things* than *saying things.* I'll go FUCKING NUTS in here and you'll all be sorry about it! I'm pretty sure all you're all going to do is masturbate, shit, and eat sandwiches forever!" Then Blaine pointed to one of the bathroom stalls. "And didn't anyone notice that Robert just dragged Jordy into one of the stalls and is fucking him in the mouth right now?"

Moaning and slurping noises came from the stall.

Blaine looked disgusted. "I'm not even sure if that kid is 18!! I'm sick of this! Sick of the laziness! Sick of the perversion! I'm getting out of here and you should all come with me!" He stood defiantly, as if he was all in-your-face about it, getting ready to leave with or without everyone. "All right, I'm going," he said. "Now who's coming with me?"

Robert started shouting from the bathroom stall. "I'm CUMMING!! I'm CUMMING!! Oh my god, it feels so good! Swallow Daddy's load, boy!"

Amy laughed, and said, "That's *ONE* I guess."

"Me too," said Kevin (the main Kevin, the only Kevin who wants to cut himself loose from all these other Kevins finally and leave them all behind.) *I could even be one of these main characters and get to talk a lot more,* he thought. *Hmmmm, that would be nice.*

Hey! That's what I *want to do!* Sean thought back, as if hearing Kevin's thoughts somehow.

Sean spoke up and said, "Me t—," but was immediately cut-off by Amy.

"Well, Kevin, if you're going, I'm going," she said.

Oh, you BITCH! Sean thought at her.

"Even though you puked on my tits and wouldn't fuck me," she continued, "you still bandaged me up after I was almost burned to death by Mr. Coffee and that was very nice of you and stuff." Then she looked down at his crotch, and added, "Plus, you have a penis. And I like those."

"Okay, that's two," Blaine said. "Excluding Robert, who was just fucking someone in the mouth when he said he was coming."

"Hey, I said I was coming too," Sean tried to say, but was quickly cut off again.

"*Jordy cumming too!* Jordy cumming *everywhere!* It feels so good!" Jordy shouted from the stall, super-retarded like.

"Again, what I said before," Blaine noted, like he was the only smart one in the room all of a sudden.

"I'll come if Jordy comes," Chip said. "He's the strongest of us and I know he'll protect me. And I don't care what he does in private with old men, that's his choice. And I like being carried on his back. It makes me feel tall."

"*I* want to be carried on Jordy's back!" Amy complained. "That's *not fair!*"

Kevin put his hand on Amy's shoulder, "But Mimi, Chip is crippled. He can't use his legs. He needs all the help he can get." Kevin looked at Chip, and said, "You're a brave little kid, Chip."

Chip smiled, "My mom says it's okay to be crippled, as long as you have a lot of courage!" he said, retardedly.

"That's right," Kevin said, kneeling down to give Chip a nice pat on the head.

"Then let's get going, already," Dan said.

"Yeah, what are we waiting for!" asked Dave, with an exclamation point instead of a question mark.

"Hey guys, I'm still here too, remember?" Sean said. "*But you all just keep ignoring me!*"

Blaine gave him a look. "Didn't you die?" he asked.

Before he could answer, Judith jumped up and pounced on him like a cougar, grabbing his arm. "If Sean's going then count me in!" she said, excitedly.

Robert came out of the bathroom in his underwear, carrying Jordy on his back wearing nothing but his helmet.

"Jordy and Robert coming too!" Jordy said.

Robert looked at them all and said, "All right Troops! Let's get the hell out of here!"

Blaine, Kevin, Amy, Dan/Dave, Chip, Robert, Jordy, Sean, and Judith walked out of there, with Robert leading the way.

"They're all going to die out there horribly, torn apart by machines all over the hotel," Horny Kevin said to Pervert Kevin.

"Yeah," he agreed. "I bet every room in here is a death trap now except for this one."

"They should've just stayed here and had sandwiches."

"*Totally.*"

Then the room exploded and every sandwich, Kevin, and every other person with mono were destroyed all at once.

A kid in a wheelchair appeared in there, too late.

CHAPTER CYBORG

Kevin grabbed the map posted on the wall next to the elevators, and tore it off. Then he laid it down on the ground and everyone gathered around it like they were the Goonies. And that's what it felt like because they had all seen that movie and were big fans. It was eventually decided that they should make their way through to the atrium, a part of the hotel only containing trees and ponds.

(Probably full of coins too—maybe One-Eyed Willy's treasure! —the Narrator)

They thought it would be their best bet, since there probably weren't as many machines in there as there would be in the arcade, gym, laundry room, and kitchen—which were all on the way to the atrium.

(That's the stupidest line of reasoning *ever!* I bet they will all die in a ridiculously contrived way, like in alphabetical order. —the Narrator)

And since a hallway leads to the atrium, there would be no reason to go into any of these places to get killed. And they won't even have to go into the basement for any reason whatsoever.

Kevin pressed the door to the elevator.

Blaine flipped out.

(Because Kevin was pressing the *door* to the elevator and not the *button* to the elevator? Holy shit, Blaine is *smart.* —the Narrator)

"Holy shit, bro! What the fuck are you doing!?" Blaine screamed. "The elevator is a fucking machine! We have to take the stairs, dude!"

Judith disagreed, "Now wait just a minute, young man.

I don't know how many stories up we are, but I don't want to be walking down a bunch of stairs now. I'm a little old lady, you know. I think we should wait for the elevator and see if it's fine. It just might be." Judith turned to face the elevator, like everyone agreed with her. "Besides," she said, "I snorted a bunch of meth earlier and I feel like shit."

Blaine was dumbfounded, "It could be some kind of torture chamber! It could kill us all! I bet you anything when those doors open it's going to be something very, *very* bad, like a death trap, or some kind of torture chamber!"

"Yeah, like in *Hellraiser 2*," Kevin remembered, suddenly reminiscing about one of his favorite movies to his brother, "There was that terrifying torture chamber thing in hell that came up like an elevator and grabbed that guy and turned him into the most *badass* crazy guy EVER!"

"That was a horror movie, dude. With fantasy elements," Dan interjected. "This is reality. It would be more like that insane super-computer thing that turned that chick into a killer cyborg at the end of *Superman III*."

"But I don't remember anything about that movie," Kevin said, like it was unimportant.

"Well, I do!" Blaine screamed. "It was horrible!"

"Yeah!" Kevin said. "So shut up, Dan, or Dave, or whatever the fuck your name is."

They can HEAR ME? Dave said to himself.

The elevator dinged and the doors opened, without anyone having pressed the button.

Inside, the walls were covered in elaborate computer-chip panels blinking with colored lights. There were tons of cables and wires snaking all over, throbbing and shooting sparks. Robotic arms and sharp metal stabby things hung from the ceiling, making scary noises.

Huge metal coils reached out and grabbed Judith. They pulled her inside so quickly she didn't even have a second to bitch about it. The coils held her in place, and metal arms and computer wires pierced her skin with their pointy metal ends, fusing machine parts to her. Metal panels were slapped onto every inch of her body and screwed on. The rewiring took over her brain, turning her into a horrifying robot cyborg.

"Holy shit! Dave was right!" Blaine screamed.

Dan panicked. *GASP*, he thought. *They can HEAR Dave!*

"Oh my god, movies are real!" Dan screamed, thinking that Dave must be real too. (He knew he was!)

"Even *Superman III*?" Kevin asked.

"Yes!! Even the stupidest movie ever!" Blaine shouted.

"What happened in the movie?"

"She started killing everybody!"

They looked scared. Especially Sean, who looked like he was going to shit his pants. Other people had reactions as well but there's no time to describe them all.

The cyborg opened its metallic silver eyes and walked out of the elevator, stomping along on heavy metal feet.

"What the fuck should we do?!" Blaine screamed, panicking. "She's going to start shooting death rays at everyone or something!"

"Give her Sean! She wanted to fuck him earlier!" Dan/Dave replied.

Sean gasped, betrayed. "But I haven't even been fleshed-out as a character yet and given anything to do!"

Blaine grabbed him by the shoulders, and said, "Then here's your chance!"

Blaine shoved Sean at the Judith Cyborg. She grabbed him by nipples and twisted them until they tore off. Wires shot out of her chest and shredded his clothes. Then she lifted him off the ground and held him in place while she zapped his naked, nippleless body again and again with a scary blue death laser.

(The sounds effects sounded like this – "ZzzzACK! ZzzzAP! CrrrACK!" plus Luke Skywalker screaming in *Return of the Jedi* —the Narrator)

The metal monstrosity dropped Sean's smoking hot body onto the ground. It was smoking hot because he was on fire. She started doing unspeakable things to him with electrified wires and glistening metal instruments. A lot of crazy bad things went up his butt. Some of them came out of his mouth. His eyeballs shot out as wires exploded through his eye sockets. His body stretched and tore apart. Sean writhed in his death throes.

(That's so cliché! —the Narrator)

"EVERYONE RUN FOR THE STAIRS!!!" Robert said, finally interjecting. (Robert doesn't watch a lot of movies.)

More living machines from the other rooms burst into the hall, like the weird amalgam from the seminar on *How to Stop Being Crippled, Retarded, Insane, or Gay*, and the killer tanning bed machine from the seminar on *How to Stop Being Old*. Neither seminar had turned out to be successful in curing anyone or helping anybody out like promised.

But on the other hand, the *Mono Singles Mixer* kind of went alright, save for a few dead Kevins.

More and more machines filled the hallway—machines shooting stale sandwiches, computer screens flashing that dumb *Matrix* coding, tiny cellphone robots with scorpion tails, television monitors playing Vince Kramer's head surgery; everything you can think of. Some machines were combined with corpses and skeletons, making them look even more terrifying.

Everyone made it to the stairwell at the last second. As they shut the door behind them, Jesus peered out from behind the door for the *Gay Retard Seminar*, lurking there, watching everyone flee to safety. He sneered like he was up to something.

At the other end of the hall, Andrew, the autistic kid, watched as well.

(Those guys are *definitely* up to something. —the Narrator)

The group emerged from the stairwell into the hall on the bottom level, quickly checking to see if their lives were still with them. They were.

After a brief sigh of relief, Sean was decapitated by a flying saw blade. A fountain of blood shot up from his neck while his arms flailed around, comically searching for his head. Even though they were all *totally* hoping they wouldn't run into any more machines, there were more in the lobby at the end of the hall. It was utter pandemonium in there.

(You mean *brouhaha.* —the Narrator)

Yes, there was a major *brouhaha* going on in the lobby, with wild machines running all over killing people and destroying the hotel's fancy ten million dollar renovation from the late 70s. A tool-shop machine had been busy ripping down the old wallpaper when it noticed the group in the hall and started shooting saw blades at them. The machine behind it was busy stapling sheets of human skin to the wall, while another splashed bucketfuls of blood all over it. The new décor was coming along nicely.

Behind the front desk, the clerk was shooting randomly at things with a shotgun. When he noticed the group, he screamed for help. "Oh my god, help me!" he yelled. "This is worse than sitting through a new Stephen King mini-series every summer!"

Everyone ignored him and ran across the lobby to the hall to the atrium.

"What about Sean?!" Dan/Dave asked.

"He's dead, leave him!" Blaine commanded, thinking Dan was being a stupid little bitch for caring about someone who died a long time ago.

Unfortunately the hall to the atrium was full of cyborg people from the elevators just like Judith. They walked back and forth erratically while randomly shooting laser blasts at nothing in particular. Upholstery machines were busy tearing up the carpet. Vacuum cleaners raced across the ceiling, tearing it apart. And a machine using a severed human arm as a paintbrush was writing "FUCK YOU" all over the walls.

Chip squeezed tighter to Jordy's back, because that's where he's been this whole time. "How are we going to get through all of *that*, Jordy? I'm scared!" Chip cried.

"Don't worry, Chip! You can wear my special helmet!"

Jordy sat Chip on the carpet and put his helmet on him. Jordy was still naked though, so his enormously-sized retard penis accidentally smacked Chip across the face.

Chip paid it no attention. He was just excited that he was getting to wear Jordy's special helmet. "Yay!" he exclaimed.

"Now you're *super-strong!* Just like Jordy! Nothing can hurt you now! You're brave! The *bravest* little kid ever!" Jordy said excitedly.

"Exactly!" Chip smiled. "It's like I said earlier, it's okay to be handicapped as long as you have a lot of courage!"

Jordy grabbed him by the legs.

Chip's enthusiasm suddenly withered away. "Hey, what are you doing?" he asked, worried.

"Be brave, Chip!" Jordy said.

Jordy pulled Chip up by the ankles and ran at all the machines in the hallway with him, swinging Chip around like a big retarded human weapon.

Chip screamed his head off. It was not fun.

The group was pleasantly surprised with this turn of events. And better Chip than any of them.

"Come on, guys! Follow Jordy!" Blaine said.

Jordy swung Chip so hard at a cyborg that its head went flying off. Jordy kicked over the body and moved on. But a vacuum cleaner detached from the ceiling to get him. It landed on the ground upright and Jordy smashed it with Chip's body like he was a human baseball bat. The vacuum cracked open and started smoking, giving off that awful smell a vacuum cleaner does when it runs over a rubber band.

Chip was still screaming so the "special helmet" seemed to be helping him maintain consciousness.

But all the machines in the hall had *seriously* taken notice of them and moved in for the kill.

Jordy shouted back to the group, "Run! Hide! I'll take care of all these machines! And I'll catch up to you all in a minute!" not sounding that retarded *at all.*

(Maybe retards are people too. —the Narrator)

(Yeah, I think that's the message I've been going for here. —Vince Kramer)

Jordy ran down the hall swinging his human weapon, causing as much damage as possible to their robotic foes. At this point Chip was even going '*weeeeee!*', even though it's possible it was because he was suffering from massive brain damage.

Everyone ran into the closest open room. Kevin paused at the doorway to look back. Jordy seemed to disappear into the crowd of machines. They had enveloped him completely— as if he was just eaten up by them. Kevin seriously doubted that Jordy and Chip would survive, but silently thanked them for trying to save them all. Hopefully this room would be a safe place for them to sit tight, and their sacrifice would be worth it.

Unfortunately, that room was the arcade.

Probably not the safest place to be.

CHAPTER
ROBOTRON

The arcade looked like the best place ever. Probably the *funnest* place to be. It sounded as loud as a Tokyo casino, but with fun video game noises instead of annoying slot machine ones and J-Pop blaring.

Blaine got excited and started bouncing off the walls, but not literally. "Holy shit!" he said, all excited. "This place has *everything*! Look at all the vintage games! WOW! They've got *Space Invaders*, *Frogger*, *Ground Kontrol*, *Q-Bert*, *Gattaca*, and even those really cool old animated ones – *Dragon's Lair* and *Space Ace*! *I loved those!"*

(Gattaca? I didn't know that movie was based on an old 80s video game. Cool. —the Narrator)

"And holy shit – *LOOK!"* Blaine continued, "They've got all five *Mortal Kombat* games in a row next to each other! ALL FIVE, including the last one - *Mortal Kombat 4*! And they got all the newer shit too, like *Pac-Man: Battle Royale*, *Battle Royale: Centipede*, *House of the Dead: The Movie*, *Battle Royale: Pac Man vs. Centipede*!" But then Blaine noticed a really old vintage game he had never heard of before. "*Robotron*?" he asked. "I've never heard of that before."

The wild graphics, blinking lights, and sound effects drew him in closer to the game, as if he was entranced by it.

The group noticed this happening, and putting all their common sense together, realized the arcade games were probably all extremely dangerous and rushed to go pull him away from it.

They grabbed him, but it was too late. A shiny blue transporter beam shone on them, and they were digitized and sucked into the game, pixel by pixel.

Jesus' path in the hallway was suddenly blocked by Andrew, the autistic kid. The one in the wheelchair. The one that didn't *need* to be in a wheelchair, but was in one anyway because something ominous was happening to him or something.

"Get the fuck out of my way, *retard*," Jesus said, not looking at him directly.

Andrew didn't move.

"Oh, fuck you, kid," Jesus said, and trudged forward. Jesus tried to go around him but the wheelchair went *sideways* to block his path. "What the fuck?" Jesus asked.

"Fuck," Andrew said. "What the fuck."

"I don't have time for this, you annoying little shit," Jesus raised his hand to strike him.

"I wouldn't do that if I were you," Andrew said.

"Or what?" Jesus asked.

"Or you'll be sorry," Andrew implied.

As a person with Asperger's Syndrome, Jesus knew it was always better to be safe than sorry. He put his hand down.

Andrew just kept staring at him. It was giving Jesus the creeps. He didn't know what to say in this situation. After a while, he decided he should just ask, "What the fuck are you looking at, kid?" not really expecting a response.

"I am looking at *you*, Jesus. Do you know what's going on out there?" Andrew asked.

"No, and I don't really give a fuck either. I just want to—"

Andrew cut him off. "They're burning our world, Jesus. And some malevolent force is watching it burn. And as they watch, I watch. I'm watching it burn."

Jesus was dumbfounded. But deep down he always knew something like this would happen. His demeanor changed. "But, why?" Jesus asked.

Andrew glared at him from his wheelchair. "Because there are too many who have no reason to live. And something has to clean it up."

Jesus was taken aback.

That was pretty fucked up.

Robotron was a two-dimensional game set a hundred years in the future where robots had taken over the world. In that time, they have killed every living human being left on Earth save but one family of five. But now those five people were Kevin, Blaine, Robert, Dan/Dave and Amy.

Only one person had a gun, and was supposed to protect the other people from the robots, who were defenseless. All the stupid robots had to do was touch a person, and they'd be exploded.

Kevin ended up being the one re-digitized into the game world with the gun in his hand. Unfortunately, unlike his brother Blaine, Kevin had never much liked video games, nor was he very good at them.

Blaine shouting at him, telling him what to do, didn't help either.

The robots got everyone one-by-one. First Robert was gone, then Blaine disappeared, and when Dan/Dave was shot, he split in two and blipped out of the game. Amy seemed to last the longest, pulling off some sweet dodging moves. But they eventually got her, too.

Kevin didn't knew if any of them were really dead, or just video game dead. But he now stood alone against the machines as the last person on Earth.

"You...you *talk to them*?" Jesus asked.

Andrew just nodded.

"Where is this going, then? Have they told you?" Jesus inquired.

"They have told me everything. I speak to them. I speak to them even now. Every machination, every *movement* – it's all *language*. And I understand language. I understand language in *all things*. Even things most would deem dismissible. It is all the patchwork of something beyond our greater understanding."

Jesus got pissed off. "Well then understand *this*, you little fuck! I—"

"Your syndrome creates a shield for you that stops you from processing all of this. Your selfishness and hatred of all others will be your downfall. You need to look at the way you process things in a completely different manner. You have created an imaginary bubble for yourself, but it is not impenetrable. It will burst, and you will burst with it. But with your syndrome, you have the ability to cope. You... *actually* have the ability to do many great things. You just have to open your mind."

Jesus was at a loss for words again.

"Jesus. *Open your mind...*" Andrew closed his eyes and reached out to touch him.

(Like the fucking mutant from *Total Recall*? Hey, I saw that movie. You guys gonna make the fucking sky blue again by getting to the reactor or what here? —the Narrator)

Jesus gasped. That's what it reminded him of, too. That movie scared the fuck out of him. He took his chance and finally ran past Andrew to escape.

At the doorway to the stairwell, he turned back and shook his fist at Andrew. "*FUCK YOU!*" Jesus yelled, "I'm going to get out of here and far away from all you fucking retards, and I'll kill anyone who gets in my way!" Jesus turned and ran down the stairs. But then he quickly came back for a second and shouted, "I'm horny as hell, too! You're lucky I didn't grab you and fuck you in the mouth!"

It wouldn't be the first time Jesus grabbed a little kid and fucked him in the mouth. It wouldn't have even been the first time Jesus raped someone in a wheelchair. Jesus was a sick fucking pervert.

(Bet you didn't know Jesus was a sick fucking child-molesting rapist pervert, huh? —the Narrator)

Jesus ran down the stairs again and quickly came back to yell one last thing, "If I ever see you or any of those other fucking retards again, *I'LL FUCKING KILL YOU!*"

(And a murderer too. —the Narrator)

Then Jesus turned away and ran down the stairs again. Andrew waited for him to come back for a little while, assuming he would. When he didn't, Andrew pressed the controls on the wheelchair and faded away. He had stuff to do. Things were falling into place.

Robert was trapped in a Civil War game called, *You're Trapped in the Civil War*. Fortunately, he *could* kill people with his mind in the gamescape. It was awesome. He had never been happier. Actually, he could do that for the rest of his life. He would never need to leave. He could be happily trapped in the game forever.

Blaine was stuck in *Mortal Kombat*. Even though he had beaten the game a million times, he almost pissed himself when Scorpion said, *"GET OVER HERE!"* and threw that crazy scorpion-rope sharp thing at him. Blaine quickly ducked, and looked up to see the video game character nearly on top of him with a flying downward kick. Blaine covered his head and curled up into a ball.

Dan/Dave were trapped in *Gattaca*. Separated, Dan was an Ethan Hawke-sort-of-douche and Dave was a crippled, whiny British person in a wheelchair. They started arguing about DNA strands and fighting over who got to fuck Gwyneth Paltrow.

(I think Vince meant, Uma Thurman. But I'd bet that they'd rather fuck Gwyneth Paltrow, anyway, even though she wasn't in that movie. –the Narrator)

(I don't know, I think Uma Thurman is pretty hot. –the Editor)

Amy was trapped in a game called *Minimum Underdrive*. In it, machines were taking over the world, but she and the main characters didn't have enough energy to do anything about it, so they sat around eating sandwiches and drinking tea. Amy grabbed a sandwich and took a seat near the coffee table and plugged the Mr. Coffee machine into her spine. She hummed as if it was replenishing all of her energy.

Jordy jumped back in the room and stopped all the arcade machines from killing everybody by going to WinCo to go buy beer before the cut-off time so he could crack one open to get out of his mental rut.

Actually, Vince Kramer did that. But he went to McDonald's first to use their wi-fi so he could check his bank account, which thankfully had just been replenished with new PayPal money. At WinCo, he encountered strange night people he didn't like, and was extremely afraid of leaving his iPad in his car unguarded. A skanky chick with lots of luggage blocking the door asked him if she could have his cigarette when he was done with it. No, Vince Kramer is never one to throw away an unfinished cigarette. He smokes it all the way to the butt until it's gone, because he's not a wasteful bitch carrying a lifetime of baggage and childhood trauma. Vince was raised with better values than that. After he was done smoking, he quickly got his beer and left, happy to see his iPad was still in his car and it had not been broken into. On the way home, two pedestrians wandered into the street in front of him, not even caring that a speeding car was coming. He had to slow down for them, which pissed him off. Really pissed him off. But that was pretty normal in his neighborhood. This always shocked Vince because he was raised to look both ways before crossing the street, like a normal person. And if a car was coming, he would fucking run for it to the other side of the road to safety so he wouldn't fucking die. But anyway, Vince got home and cracked open a Pyramid Outburst, poured it into a nice pint glass he got at BizarroCon, and listened to Raped by the Beast *by Cannibal Corpse, plotting his next move.*

A few months later, when Vince was doing the second draft of this book, he coincidentally went to WinCo at the same time he did at this point in the story to go grab some more beer to drink. He had become a heavy alcoholic the last few months and needed beer to do anything, even write. But when he came home he listened to Pressure by Billy Joel instead of death metal, reminiscing about his youth, which seemed even further away ever since he had turned 35.

Dream Warriors by Dokken came up on his iPod next. It was the best song ever. He was glad that Dokken didn't die in that plane crash that week. That would've sucked.

Anyone ever wonder if Pat Benatar is on welfare now? She looks like it.

Jordy was alive, victorious against the machines blocking their path in the hallway. Chip, however, was not. It took Jordy a while to realize that he had died, and kept talking to him throughout the whole fight.

When Jordy realized that Chip was dead, he couldn't stop crying. He had killed him. "Jordy, bad!" he screamed. "Jordy, *bad!*"

He took his blood-smeared helmet off of Chip. Chip's brains sloshed out of it. Jordy shook it out, sobbing. "No more brains!" and put it back on his retarded head. Then he pounded his fist on his helmet, crying, "Jordy has no brains either!" he said retardedly. "Jordy *bad!*" he said over and over a few more times while pounding his fist on his head.

He griefstrickenly walked to the room he had left the group. It would have been more exciting to tell them all how he saved the day if he hadn't accidentally killed Chip. He almost thought about not telling them that, maybe just saying the machines got him and there was nothing he could do! But he knew better than to lie about it. He was raised to learn the consequences of a lie could get you beaten repeatedly in the head.

So, he grabbed Chip's corpse by the ankle and dragged it along, ready to face the music.

When he walked into the arcade, it was empty. Had his friends left? Had they died somehow? Jordy was confused. But then he had a thought—maybe they went into the arcade games! He walked over to one of the games, and sure enough, there was Robert on the screen, fighting for his life.

Maybe Jordy wasn't so retarded after all.

And maybe he could still save the day.

But that's when Jesus came up and grabbed him from behind, covering his mouth so he couldn't scream, and dragged him backward.

Jordy was still holding Chip's corpse and it slid with him, leaving a smear of blood along the floor.

A little boy watched all this from his hiding-spot behind an arcade game called, *Hide and Seek or DIE!*

"Okay, retard!" Jesus screamed in Jordy's ear. "Be quiet or I'll fuck you in the ass and mouth like I've been doing to the little boy I found in here. You're going to hand over the helmet, or I'll slit your throat."

But then Jesus realized he no longer had the knife he thought he had in his pocket.

The little kid had it. Jesus had been pickpocketed by a scamp! But Jesus didn't know about the kid's plan to stab him in the back until the little shit ran from behind the machine and tried to stab him in the back.

Jesus turned around at the last moment and the kid's knife plunged deep into Jordy's stomach, instead.

Jordy tried to scream but just choked up a mouthful of blood.

Jesus, shocked, let go of Jordy's body. Jordy fell to his knees clutching his stomach and spitting up blood. He fell over face first, onto his face, and drowned in a pool of his own blood.

"You little shit!" Jesus screamed, and kicked the knife out of the boy's hand.

The kid—Jimmy—screamed and ran out of the room into the hall, finally deciding to take his chances outside of the arcade where that front desk guy had left him way back at the beginning of the book.

Kevin eventually did finally beat *Robotron*, getting the highest score of *ALL TIME*. A big blinking light appeared in the sky and told him so. But before he could celebrate, he was undigitized, and shot out of the machine in a ray of blue light.

He was suddenly face-to-face with the murdering Jesus, who stood over Jordy and Chip's dead bodies all murderly-like.

Kevin had never met Jesus, *or* a murderer, so he normally would've flipped out.

But beating *Robotron* had given him a new sense of confidence. He picked up the closest weapon, Chip's small and lifeless body, and started beating the crap out of Jesus with it.

Jesus didn't die from the attack, but was very, *very* badly bruised and ran out into the hallway, defeated. Kevin would've chased after him but needed to get his friends out of the arcade games first. He had learned a secret while he was trapped in the video game.

It was a simple one—video games *aren't real*. And he knew what he had to do to get them out.

But then suddenly, the kid in the wheelchair who had attacked them in the hall appeared out of thin air, obviously teleporting there somehow.

Kevin flipped out, and screamed, "HOLY SHIT!"

The kid sensed his fear. "Do not worry," the kid said, "I am here to help. My name is Andrew. I know how to get your friends out of the machine. It is all about the coding. Put the following codes into the games they are trapped in, using the buttons and the joystick, and they will be released."

"Hey!" Kevin yelled. "I was just about to do that! I know the *blasted* codes already!"

"Sure you do," Andrew smirked at him.

"I do! I learned them when I beat *Robotron*! Have you ever beat *Robotron*, you little shit?"

"Yes. It's the easiest game in the world."

"No, it's not!"

"Yes, it is."

"No, it's not!" Kevin was seriously getting pissed off. He looked down at the mysterious kid in the wheelchair, and said, "Look, *fuck off*. I've got to put the codes into the machines."

"So, do it, then," Andrew said.

"I *will*," Kevin sneered at him.

As Kevin turned to go to the first machine, Andrew said, "Wait. I have a task for you."

Kevin gave him a *fuck off* look, and asked, "And what would that be?"

"You must go to the basement," Andrew told him, seriously. "You must go to the basement and find the reactor. You must shut down the reactor. It will stop Stephen King from writing any more novels, *ever*."

(Guess Andrew doesn't know that Stephen King died in the beginning. —the Narrator)

Kevin gave him a dismissive look like he was a retard, and said, "Okay, *sure*, whatever."

"Kevin, I'm serious," Andrew continued, "Shut down the reactor. And there will never be another Stephen King book, ever again."

"What's in it for me? Why should I go to the basement

and risk my life?" he asked.

"Because they have sandwiches," Andrew said.

Kevin had just been thinking about sandwiches, so that bit of news perked him up a little. But before he could ask what kind, the autistic kid in the wheelchair disappeared into thin air again.

Kevin put all the correct codes into the corresponding games where his friends were trapped. He freed Blaine first, then Robert, then Amy, and then Dan. They all rematerialized digitally in a blue light-ray and stood before Kevin, confused at first, but then happy to be alive. But then someone else came out, too. He looked exactly like Dan.

"Dave?" Dan asked.

Dan and Dave had been split into two separate entities.

Dave looked at everyone and said, "Game over, man!"

Dave stood in front of them, looking like Dan's exact twin. He started checking out his "new" body. He flexed and felt his muscles. He put his hand up his shirt and rubbed his hairy chest a bit. It felt good. And then he put his hand down his pants and felt his dick and balls. They felt *great.* He smiled and he laughed. He was relieved, and happy to be alive. His *own* person.

He looked back at them all again. His face turned really serious, as if he just remembered the situation they were all in. He remembered the machines. He remembered *everything.* Then he said, "Megatron must be stopped. No matter the cost."

(What? He only speaks in 80s movie quotes, and shit? —the Narrator)

It appeared that Dave could only talk using 80s movie quotes, and shit.

Blaine, who got it, and knew exactly which 80s movies Dave was quoting, pounded his fist forward and made an exciting action stance. "Fuck yeah! It's *GO TIME, BABY!"* he said, melodramatically acting like an 80s action movie star. Which is fun, so everyone should try it.

"Who the fuck is Megatron?" Amy asked Kevin.

"Are you kidding me?" Blaine interjected, looking at her like she was a dumb twat. "*Everyone* knows who Megatron is. Even *retards* know who Megatron is."

Blaine's excitement was a little contagious to Kevin, and he was about to turn to Amy to say something like, "Yeah! In your FACE!"

But before he could, Robert freaked out and screamed, "*THAT'S PROBABLY THE BASTARD WHO'S BEHIND THIS WHOLE DIRTY MESS!* FUCK YEAH! LET'S FIND THIS MEGATRON AND FUCK HIM IN HIS FUCKING ASS!!"

He also meant, *stop him*, but maybe fucking whoever is behind this whole mess in the ass also wouldn't hurt. I mean, no one argued with him about it.

CHAPTER
THE BASEMENT

"This is finally getting better," Kevin said.

"Yeah," Amy said. "I like where this is going."

"Pretty fucking awesome, if I do say so myself!" Blaine said, looking at Dave, just *really* excited about him.

Dave was looking back at him like he wanted to give him a blowjob. Dan noticed this, and felt a little jealous for some reason.

Jordy's retarded, lifeless body and Chip's crippled corpse still lay dead on the ground nearby.

Kevin motioned at them. "Wait, does anyone else care that Chip and Jordy are dead?" he asked, looking down at their corpses.

"No, not really," Blaine said. "This is the kind of crazy shit I've always dreamed of! First, I was fighting Scorpion and now *this!*" he said, referring to Dan and Dave.

Kevin sighed. He kind of figured that at this point the more people that were dead, the better. He was really coming into his own as a main character and thought it would just give him a better chance to shine.

Dan agreed with Blaine, it *was* that amazing. He finally went over and grabbed Dave and hugged him for a warm embrace. "I knew you were real!" Dan said, "*All these years*, you weren't just a part of me for no reason. You're as real as I am! I'm *NOT* crazy!" He smiled, realizing how important that was, and said it again, "I'M NOT CRAZY! Ha-*HA!*"

Dave smiled back at Dan, excited too. "You're my friend till the end," Dave said, hugging him tight.

"*CHILD'S PLAY!*" Blaine shouted, naming the movie quote.

91

The group re-grouped—revitalized, all pretty happy, and decided their next move.

They were going to stay in the arcade and wait until everything blew-over since the machines in there were harmless and a vending machine had broken and died all over the floor and left goodies for everyone, which they sat down and enjoyed.

Machines outside the resort were still ripping the city apart. It was probably the most successful *brouhaha* of all time.

(And apparently the author thought it would be more interesting to focus on the action inside of a big gay resort and convention center instead of *that* the whole time. —the Narrator)

Even though it was chaos out there, the geeks at the *Sci-Fi & Fantasy Convention* were still having a *great* time, totally oblivious to whatever was going on in the real world. But they always are anyway, which is a blessing. They also had drinks and sandwiches. It was pretty much the best thing ever. And Nathan Fillion even stopped by! And when he freaked out about all the machines outside coming to life, killing everybody, and how he barely escaped with his life before he got there, everyone just thought he was doing a bit. *Oh, that Nathan Fillion*, everyone thought, *he's as entertaining as he is gorgeous!*

Nathan Fillion was about to cry before someone sat him down, gave him a sandwich and mixed drink and told him to relax and take a load off. Fans do sometimes understand the stress of being a celebrity, you know.

Robert had another boner.

(And he wasn't even *around* Nathan Fillion. —the Narrator)

But he also wondered why he had forgotten his purpose. He wanted a cure. He wanted to be righted. Did he want to be young again? Stop being retarded? Meet other singles? He forgot why he was there in the first place. And did he even want to kill people with his mind anymore? He wasn't sure what he wanted to do before this all had happened. He was also starting to think that he wasn't even a conqueror of the Civil War, or an old man of a hundred and eighty years. He could just be some sort of okay person, maybe in his seventies. Probably a pervert, or a retard (which sometimes come with senility anyway), but he was still a *human being*.

And that wasn't so bad.

(Yeah it is. Being a perverted, senile retard is horrible. —the Narrator)

Blaine wished he had his phone so he could take photos of Dan and Dave and post about how awesome it was on Facebook. He actually got a bit depressed about it, even though things *were* amazing. But it didn't matter in that moment. It felt like it was the end of the world. So he sulked, realizing that he might not be able to use Facebook *ever again*. It kind of just made him want to die. And if he ever made it back to the outside world, it would just be a destroyed ruin. And in a world without Facebook, he thought, it might as well be, anyway.

Dan and Dave were sitting down together talking. Dan reveled in the fact that Dave only responded in 80s movie quotes from their youth that they had always enjoyed watching together. And it was no coincidence that they had all the same favorites, so it was really great for Dan. But Dave was kind of more like his brother now.

His *twin* brother.

Dan had always wanted a brother, so Dave always did, too. It was comforting for both of them. Dan had never been happier.

The world might have been going to shit, but all of his dreams were coming true. And when Dave started singing the theme to *The Karate Kid Part II* to him (the one that went, "Like a knight in shining armor, from a long time ago!"), it only made Dan happier.

Kevin reflected back on everything that happened and decided that while it was *exciting*, he still probably should've never left the house.

He was damned sure that something *really, really* terrible might happen next, at any moment, and one of them would probably die because of it. Even though he said to himself before that it might be okay, because he'd have more of a chance to shine, he realized he really didn't mean it. He wanted everyone to survive. He wanted to save everybody.

He thought back to what Andrew had told him about shutting down the reactor. He was starting to become pretty sure that it did something other than stop Stephen King from writing ever again.

(Not only because that would be ridiculous, since Stephen King was already dead, but also because even if he wasn't, nothing could stop him anyway. Not car crashes, not blindness, and *definitely* not Kevin. —the Narrator)

It probably did something that was worth going for.

Besides, he was told there would be sandwiches.

No one knew that Amy was a cyborg death machine robot.

Whatever was left in Amy died with the burns she got from Mr. Coffee. The machine had torn out her heart and soul and replaced the blood in her veins with hot coffee. She was a pretender amongst them. A deadly killing machine. Waiting for the right moment to strike.

There's not enough sandwiches in the world to make something like that all better.

(Sandwiches really are the best thing ever. Let me tell you all about them. Sometimes, I make several sandwiches at once, only using the finest meat, so I have enough to last me for a whole week. I like to dip them in oil sometimes. Sesame, olive, it doesn't matter; they just taste so good that way. Every single bite. It's like a mouth orgasm. And filling, too! There are many ways to eat sandwiches, and many ways to make them, but I make them the best and I live a full life because I do that. You all could learn a lot from me, you know. Holy shit, I need another beer. I have a book to write. —Vince Kramer)

"I'm really, *really* bipolar, you know," Blaine said to his brother, Kevin, who wished they were eating sandwiches with each other. "I mean," he continued, "I know sometimes I seem like a real nice and fun guy. *Wild*, even. Fun to be around. I've always taken good care of you, haven't I, dude?"

Kevin thought about it, a little mad the conversation obviously wasn't going to be about sandwiches, and said, "I guess."

"But I also haven't," Blaine said. "I've been horrible. I've been a drain on our family and you don't deserve that. There is such… just such… *I don't know*. There's something in me that shouldn't be there. I know I do my best to hide it. But it's a big struggle for me."

Kevin always had his own ordeals too, but Blaine's actions and meltdowns had always seemed to make him get more attention in the family. Kevin always just shrugged it off. The less attention on him, the better, he thought. "That's okay," Kevin reassured him.

"But it's *not*," Blaine argued. "Not for you. It's not good enough for you. And I'm sorry. I'm sorry about what happened to you, Kevin. I'm sorry what happened when we were kids."

Lots of bad things had happened when they were kids. So Kevin didn't really know what he could be talking about.

Blaine frowned, and almost started to cry. "I wish... *I just wish*. I could've been stronger," he said. He looked at Kevin apologetically, tears rolling down his face. "I'm *so sorry*, Kevin."

Kevin looked at him, unworried. Kind of wishing he could give him a sandwich right now to shut him up. "That's okay," Kevin said, ignoring whatever dramatic issue his brother was bringing up. He was used to it. He put his hand on Blaine's shoulder, and again, wished he could give him a sandwich.

Blaine got a bit angry at that and smacked his hand away from him, and got up and ran off crying.

That does it, Kevin thought. *We have to get out of this room.*

It took a while, but Kevin convinced everyone to go on the "start the reactor" quest with him to the basement. He told them there would be sandwiches, whiskey, board games, and pornographic magazines. Oh, and that there was a kill switch that would stop all the machines once and for all. "And besides," he said, "it would be fun. Wouldn't you guys like an adventure?"

The answers were, "Kind of," "Not really," and "Sure. Why not?"

(And I also would've added "Anything to move the story along." —the Narrator)

(Shut up, you're not writing this book. —Vince Kramer)

(I could write my own book. —the Narrator)

(Yeah? What would it be called? The Flight of the Narrator? What would it be about? A big fucking retard who likes to interrupt everything and state the obvious? —Vince Kramer)

(I don't know. *Maybe?* —the Narrator)

(Shut up, or I will DELETE YOU! —Vince Kramer)

(... —the Narrator)

Everyone forgot what they were doing for a second.

The group finally piled into the hallway, which was devoid of machines.

Kevin got out his map and found out where the basement was. The door to it was right across the hall from the arcade and had the word, *Basement*, written on it big red letters.

When Dave noticed this, he said, "Why, there's no basement in the Alamo!"

Kevin tried to open the door. It was locked. He tried it again, because he was probably mistaken. It was still locked. He tried it a *third* time, almost positive it would open now. It didn't.

He paced back and forth three times in the hall and tried the door again. Still locked.

Kevin was getting frustrated.

At that moment, the machines started coming back. They were coming from both ends of the hall, leaving them trapped, with no escape.

(Except for back into the arcade, you know —the Narrator)

"HEY, YOU GUYS!" Dave said. *"They're hee-eere!"*

Kevin tried the door again, this time jostling it in a panic.

"Step aside!" Amy said.

Kevin stepped aside.

"Let me try," she said, and casually opened the door like it was no big deal.

Kevin was shocked, and ecstatic. He kissed her on the cheek, and said, "You're my good luck charm, Mimi!"

Amy didn't even try to correct him that her name wasn't Mimi.

"Follow me, guys!" Kevin said, leading them into the basement.

"Let's make like a tree and get outta here!" Dave said, all happy.

Kevin, Amy, Robert, Blaine, Dan, and Dave went down the stairs into the basement. When the machines got to the door, they stopped and backed off a little, as if they were afraid of it.

The group descended into the darkness down a long flight of stairs. It was actually a normal-length flight of stairs, not too long or too short, but it's better for the story if you think of it as being long and dark.

Kevin fumbled around for a light switch, accidentally grabbing one of Amy's breasts and trying to flick her nipple up-and-down to turn the lights on. Surprisingly, they did, and then Kevin realized he was playing with Amy's boobs. "Oh, sorry Mimi," he said.

She laughed, "Looks like the lights weren't the *only* thing you were trying to turn on."

The group looked at the newly-lit room. It was an old 70s discoteque. An array of colored lights came on and the silver disco ball on the ceiling started to spin. Everything was covered in dust and cobwebs, and the room smelled very musty and old. But otherwise, it was pretty awesome. *You Dropped a Bomb on Me* by The Gap Band suddenly started playing on the stereo system. And that was *really* awesome.

(Because it's the best song ever. —the Narrator)

"HOLY SHIT! *I LOVE THIS ONE!*" Blaine yelled, so everyone could hear him.

"EH?" Robert grunted, trying to hear him. This was not his generation of music. But, he couldn't remember what type of music was popular in the Civil War, anyway. It had been so long ago.

"FUCK YEAH, MAN!" Dan shouted. "DAVE, LETS KICK IT OLD SCHOOL LIKE WE USED TO!"

Dave smiled, knowing exactly what he was talking about.

"Nobody puts Baby in a corner!" Dave said, and ran out to the dance floor with Dan. They started doing their old breakdancing routine that won "them" the talent show in 2nd grade. Amy, Blaine and Kevin watched in amusement. It was a great break from almost getting killed all the time.

"KEVIN!" Blaine yelled at Kevin, who was standing right next to him. "HOW COME YOU AND ME NEVER DID THAT BACK IN THE DAY?!"

Kevin just shook his head, knowing he would never find an appropriate answer to explain why. He was just too awkward back in those days. Then he remembered something, "BLAINE!" he shouted, "I'M HUNGRY, I WAS TOLD THERE WOULD BE SANDWICHES DOWN HERE SOMEWHERE."

"WHAT?" Blaine shouted back.

"SANDWICHES!" Kevin yelled as loud as he could.

Then the record started skipping, stuck on the part where The Gap Band sang the lyric, "You dropped a bomb on me". But it almost wasn't noticeable since that line is sung a total of forty times in that song.

Then the disco ball fell to the ground and exploded.

Dan and Dave screamed, writhing on the ground, shards of glass sticking out of their faces and arms.

Kevin and Blaine ran over to help them, but the jukebox started shooting records at them. One hit Blaine between the eyes. It wasn't all that damaging, but it hurt really bad, nonetheless.

"OW!" he yelled. "That hurt *REALLY BAD!*"

Kevin kept dodging the flying records as well as he could, then dropped to the lit floor, and crawled over to the record player, intent on stopping it.

The jukebox grew wiry legs and arms, grabbed the stereo and mounted it on top of itself as if it were a head. Then it grabbed a cassette tape and put it in, and said, "DO YOU GUYS WANT TO HEAR MY NEW DEMO TAPE? I WAS CRANKING IT ON A BOOM BOX AT THE BEACH LAST WEEK AND EVERYONE REALLY SEEMED TO LIKE IT."

It pressed play and grabbed the two biggest speakers nearby and came at them, holding the speakers outright so they could get a full-blast of the music.

Even though they were all probably about to die, the music actually wasn't all that bad.

The machine was upon Kevin when Dan and Dave got up, ignoring their wounds, and started circling the thing. Dan grabbed one of the speakers and threw it. Dave grabbed the other one and bashed its head in with it.

"PLEASE!" it screamed. "I JUST WANT MY BAND TO GET DISCOVERED."

Its face broke easily because it was made of cheap plastic from the 70s. Dave grabbed it, tore it off and smashed it through its glass jukebox chest. It crackled with electricity, smoked and fell over.

Dave looked down at it, smiling. He said, "DEATH BY STEREO!"

Everyone cheered.

"Are you guys okay?" Kevin asked.

"Sure," Dan said. "We've gotten more banged up than THIS breakdancing before."

"Johnny Number Five is alive!" Dave shouted.

They were totally fine.

"Okay, good," Kevin said, getting helped up by Dan. "We've got to keep exploring the basement. I still need to find this reactor thing." He looked around. "Now if we could just find a door in this place," he murmured.

Across the room, Amy opened one, and presented the entrance to them. "Here we go, guys!" she said, happily. "I found it!"

"Way to go, Mummy!" Blaine shouted.

They all went through the door into the next room.

Unfortunately, the next room was another arcade.

Well, kind of. It was a big room full of old Commodore computers. A lot of them were the old gaming types. Different games were ready to play on each console, up on the screen, buzzing from their old floppy discs and cassette tapes.

Blaine FLIPPED OUT, remembering and recognizing all the old games immediately. And he went off, *again*.

"HOLY SHIT, GUYS!" he said, flipping out again. "They've got EVERYTHING!" He ran back and forth, pointing at everything. "LOOK! They've got all the old Sierra games! The first four *King's Quests, The Black Cauldron, Space Quest, Police Quest*; *all* the quests! Remember Kevin!? *KEVIN, YOU REMEMBER THESE, RIGHT?!*" Blaine screamed at Kevin, who was all of a sudden like *holy shit*, but not in a good way. "I haven't played any of these since we were kids! I'm going to play *King's Quest* first! Holy shit, I *loved* that game! It practically taught me to read and write! I can't wait to see it again!"

Everyone was already ready to stop him before he got to the computer. Robert put him in a headlock and Dan and Dave grabbed his arms. He struggled, intent on getting to the game.

Kevin got in his face and raised his finger up to him. "Look! We're going on a *real* quest, remember?" he said, all in-his-face-like. "Even if these old computer games *weren't* going to kill us, we definitely wouldn't have time to sit around playing them."

They let Blaine go and he shrugged them off, adjusting

his shirt. "But we'll never get a chance to play them again…" Blaine said.

"You haven't for thirty years," Dan interjected. "I think you've been able to live without them the whole time."

"Yeah," Kevin said. "I understand the need for nostalgia, I do. I love it, too. But do you really want to be killed by a witch and put into a cauldron? Do you want to be burned alive by a dragon? Do you really want to wait for minutes on end for each screen to load just to see how you're going to die next?"

Blaine almost wanted to say *maybe…* but went with, "I guess not." He got all sad again, and looked at Dave, who had a big, excited smile on his face like usual. "Dude, aren't you going to say an awesome Eighty's quote?" Blaine asked, hoping it would cheer him up. "Maybe something to do with an old video game movie?"

Dave didn't hesitate, and said with a smile, "I love the Power Glove. It's so bad!"

"FUCK YEAH!" Blaine shouted. "Awesome. Thank you."

"Okay, let's get out of here. Amy found the door again," Kevin said, motioning towards Amy, who was standing by the door with it open and waiting for them.

They walked to the other side of the room to the door and nothing bad happened to them.

Well, Robert stubbed his toe on an old Magnavox Odyssey that some jerk kid left on the ground. But that was about it.

And the funny thing was, he actually remembered *Pong*.

The next room was a *very old* laundry room. But it looked like it had been used a lot in recent years because the walls were covered in Stephen King posters. Both from his movies *and* his books. And the floor was littered with skeletons.

Robe-covered skeletons—all dusty and covered in cobwebs. It was like some kind of weird Stephen King cult used to worship down there, and then one day decided to commit mass-suicide.

(Probably because *The Dark Tower IV: Wizard and Glass* took so long to come out. —the Narrator)

But the *really* scary part was that there was a gigantic antique industrial laundry-pressing machine in the center of the room, with the number 6 on it. *Exactly* like the one in *The Mangler*.

Blaine recognized it immediately. "HOLY SHIT, IT'S THE FUCKING MANGLER!" he screamed. "That movie *sucked!*"

"Really? I kind of loved it," Kevin said.

"Yeah," Dan argued, "I thought Robert Englund was used really well in it, and I loved the staircase-to-hell ending."

Blaine suddenly remembered. "Yeah," he said, stroking his chin. "That part *was* pretty cool."

Then Robert voiced the fears they were all hiding in the back of their minds. "You know it's going to come to life any second and try to kill us, right?" he said.

And as if on cue, it did.

Ben Affleck stumbled into the room for the *SyFy Fantasy Meeting* bleeding to death and fell to his knees, choking on his own blood and gasping for air.

Everyone just pointed and laughed at him.

Then he let out a faggy death rattle and fell face-first into a pool of his own blood. There was a loud, wet smack.

The ugly, monkey-looking actor farted and shit himself loudly when he died.

His death was met with thunderous rounds of applause.

Nathan Fillion, who was completely *wasted*, belched, went over to Ben Affleck's corpse and pissed on it.

The Mangler had Dave by the arm. "BOGUS!" he screamed.

Dan fell down in extreme pain. Kevin and Robert tried to pull Dave from the machine's grasp. Kevin yanked on Dave's legs as Robert punched The Mangler in its "6", assuming it was its nose. The machine let Dave go. He fell into Kevin's arms and he tried to back away with him.

But Dave was struggling. He thrashed around screaming, "Fitty dolla bill! Fitty dolla bill!"

Dan, clutching his arm, tried to calm Dave down.

Robert was smacking The Mangler around, but it was up on its wild mechanical legs, dodging every blow.

Robert sneered. He took out his cellular telephone, quickly pulling-up his *Random Kill* app. "Take this, you motherfucking bastard!" Robert said, pressing the button.

The machine snatched Robert's phone out of his hand and crushed it to pieces.

"Aaaa*Aaaargh*, you *fuck!*" Robert screamed.

The Mangler went for the kill.

Washers and dryers along the walls shook violently, their spin cycles at *full power*. It seemed as if they were cheering.

(MANGLER! MANGLER! MANGLER! *YEAH!!!* — the Narrator)

And then Amy clapped her hands together and everything went black.

Amy clapped her hands together again, and the lights came on and everything was silent. The Mangler lay face-down on the ground, looking like a big, gay useless piece of shit, and all the washers and dryers had shut the fuck up.

Dave, clutching his broken arm, looked at her in amazement. He smiled and shouted, "It's all in the reflexes!"

She giggled, and Robert kicked The Mangler in its mangled face and said,"Take that, you *bastard!*"

Kevin assessed the situation. His conclusion was that that was all fucking awesome.

Then Jesus suddenly appeared behind Amy and put his hand over her mouth and dragged her away into the darkness.

(She was all like, "MMMmmmMMMmmmMMM!!!!!" You know, all muffled-like. Like the fucking Mummy. —the Narrator)

Kevin slung Dave onto his shoulder, grabbing his good arm, and Robert hoisted Dan to his feet. Robert had no idea why the boy was feigning an injury, since nothing had happened to him, but Kevin had a pretty good idea about what had happened.

(Since it was probably an 80s thing. 1980s, not 1880s. –the Narrator)

But Robert was still strong and invaluable to this mission. And sexy for his age, which is important.

"Robert," Kevin said. "We've got to *kill* Jesus. He's the one that killed Jordy. He's the only thing standing in the way between us and the sandwiches. And he's got *Mimi!*"

"So, are we all going to fuck her or what?" Robert asked, because it was something that he'd been wondering for a very long time.

"No," Kevin said. "But *I* might get to."

"Are you falling for her, lad?"

"*Maybe.*" He looked around the room. "Hey – where the hell is my brother?" he asked.

Blaine came up behind him and put his hand on his shoulder. "I'm here," he said. "The writer just forgot to give me anything to do in the previous scene."

"Oh, okay. Good."

They all trudged into the next room together to save

Amy, stop Jesus, eat sandwiches, and put an end to Stephen King once and for all.

(If this was an actual Stephen King book it would end right here and you would have to wait for the sequel. –the Narrator)

The next room was a big missile command computer station office that looked like it was straight from the 70s. It looked just like the one in the movie *WarGames*, starring a very-in-the-closet actor.

Blaine said, "This must be where the reactor is!"

"And the sandwiches!" Kevin said.

"And that Jesus fucker and that whore!" Robert added.

Kevin, realizing there were now three major important things to find, started having a minor panic attack because he didn't know which one to do first.

If they wasted time looking for sandwiches, they might lose Jesus and Amy. If they tried to save Amy from Jesus, they might be killed before they even had a chance to *eat* a sandwich. But if they went for the reactor first, it might solve *all* their problems *and* leave time for everything else.

Starting the reactor could also do *nothing*, which Kevin was half-expecting, and then this whole basement chapter would've all been a huge waste of time.

But then Kevin remembered he was surrounded by friends who were like his brothers at this point.

(Especially his actual brother, Blaine. –the Narrator)

Kevin looked at his brotherly-like friends, and like a leader he said, "Okay, team! Here's the plan. Blaine, you and Dave will look for the reactor. Robert and I will find Jesus and Amy. Dan, find the sandwiches. Everyone got it?"

They all nodded, except for Blaine, who raised his hand.

"Shoot," Kevin said.

"I think I already found Jesus and Amy," Blaine pointed out.

106

"Where?!" Kevin asked.

"Right behind you," Blaine said.

Kevin gasped and turned around, faced face-to-face with Jesus. Jesus had a knife at Amy's throat. Behind him lay a beautiful pile of sandwiches, on a big silver tray. A desk lamp shone on top of the platter, putting a godlike emphasis on them. And next to that, was a big red button under a glass case.

Jesus kicked Kevin in the balls.

Kevin had the wind kicked out of him. He fell to his knees grasping his balls and gasping for breath.

Robert pushed him aside. He pushed him so hard that he fell on his side and Kevin finally breathed-in. Robert raised his fist at Jesus and said, "I'm-a threaten you!"

"Oh yeah, old man?! Let's see what you got!" said Jesus.

Robert thought that meant he wanted to see how big his dick is, so he dropped trou and whipped out his big masculine man meat. He tickled his balls not once, twice, but three times, and out came the biggest cock Jesus ever had seen. It was a revelation! He had no idea they could get that big!

Amy licked her lips and went *"Mmmmmm…"* She of course had seen lots of big cocks, but this one reminded her of her father's.

The distraction was enough for Blaine, Dan, and Dave to rush Jesus. Hopefully, to put a stop to Jesus and his shit once and for all.

They were unsuccessful and two of them died.

Read about it in the next chapter.

CHAPTER
DEATH TO JESUS

Jesus threw Amy out of the way and thrust his knife out just in time to stab Dave in the heart.

It was like a big Bowie knife or something, so it totally pierced his breastplate and slid right in to that important cavity where the heart is. And the knife pierced one of the chambers in Dave's heart that you should never put knives in or you will die!

Dan clutched his chest and fell against the wall—a big 70s-like computer consol with tons of flashy buttons. He accidentally switched a lot of them on by slamming into it. LED lights lit and sounds began to whir like it was loading something.

(Probably death. —the Narrator)

"Holy shit!" Robert screamed. "Dan's having a goddamned *heart attack!*" Robert ran over to help him, his big boner hitting another switch on a counter as he rushed pass it.

Sirens and flashing red lights came on.

Dave was on top of Jesus with the knife stuck deep in his chest, coughing up blood all over Jesus' face. Jesus twisted the knife in him with an evil grin.

Dan coughed up blood all over Robert's face.

Amy ran over to Robert and grabbed his awesome cock and tried to lube it up with Dan's blood.

Blaine was over near Kevin helping him because he didn't have anything else to do right then.

108

Jesus pushed Dave off of him. He left the knife still stuck in Dave's chest.

Dave lay on his back clutching his chest because there was a big knife in it. "Bogus…" he said. And then his eyes rolled back in his head and he died.

Dan's eyes did the same and he slumped to the floor, dead as well.

"What the hell just happened?" Blaine asked his brother.

"Isn't it obvious?" Kevin said.

Blaine shook his head.

"They were connected. Whatever hurt Dave, hurt Dan," Kevin said.

"Like the twins in *Dead Ringers*?" Blaine asked.

"No, nothing like that. *At all*. Do you even remember that movie?" Kevin asked.

"Just that one part," Blaine remembered.

"Anyway," Kevin continued, "it's just like the Crimson Twins – Tomax and Xamot, from *G.I. Joe: A Real American Hero*. Whatever hurt one would hurt the other."

"OHHHHH!" Blaine's face lit-up. "I remember now! We had the action figures." Then Blaine's face got all serious. "Do you remember what happened to the action figures?" he asked his brother, who obviously was going to remember it.

"Of course," Kevin said, remembering, "That dick Matt Polito borrowed them, and then traded them to someone else for three Garbage Pail Kids cards he wanted."

"Yes," Blaine smiled. "And guess what?"

"What?" Kevin asked.

"I called the CDC the other day and had him taken away for it."

"Really?"

"Yeah."

"GOOD!"

Kevin and Blaine rejoiced. After all these years, they had finally gotten revenge on a dickhole from their childhood.

109

Everything in the Missile Command Room was coming to life. Not like, death machines of death coming to life, but powering up, blinking, and making humming and siren noises. So, maybe it was gearing up for that.

Jesus was kind of blinded by all the blood in his eyes and was staggering around trying to wipe his face off and going "Ergh. Ugh. Argh. Uh."

Amy was on top of Robert riding him like a tiger and smearing Dan's blood all over her breasts.

Blaine and Kevin took Robert's phone out of his pants to look up photos of old Garbage Pail Kids cards on the internet.

All of this went on for a little while.

Andrew appeared from out of nowhere in the middle of the room, in his floating wheelchair. But then he noticed that everyone was really busy, so he disappeared again.

Robert shot such a huge load into Amy that she went flying off his cock and slammed against the wall. She seemed to hang there suspended for a minute while his semen shot all over her face, breasts, and everything. She finally slipped in the pool of blood mixed with sperm on the floor and fell ass-first on her rear.

The last of Robert's super-strong warrior load sploshed all over the computer wall and shorted it out. It sparked and crackled. The whirring noise cut off as it powered down, and everything stopped humming and blinking.

The siren was still blaring, so Jesus ran over and flipped the switch that Robert had aroused with his amazing boner. "WHAT THE FUCK IS WRONG WITH YOU PEOPLE!?" he screamed.

110

Everyone had kind of forgotten him at this point.

That's when Robert remembered he could kill people with his mind.

Robert stood to face Jesus. Flexing his muscles. Showing off the true grit of his awesome old man strength and virile sexuality. "Back off, you bastard!" he screamed. "I will *kill you!*"

"With what, Robert?" Jesus asked. "That big dick?"

(Yeah, put that thing away before you get us all killed! —Princess Leia)

"With my *mind*, you piece of dirty crap!" Robert put his fingers to his temples and thought really, really hard at Jesus. "*Nyeeeargh!*" Robert's face reddened. He struggled to kill, knowing that somewhere, deep inside of him, he could do it just by thinking.

Jesus just laughed. "*Hahahaha!*" he went. "Is that all you've got, old man?"

Robert took a deep breath, giving up. "I used to be able to do it back in the Civil War, you know," he muttered.

"Robert," Jesus said, "You have *never* been able to kill people with your mind. You did not fight in the Civil War. You are seventy seven-years-old. And today is the day. *The day YOU DIE!*"

(Jesus knew all of this because he had taken the time to look the man up on Wikipedia. Robert was actually Robert Redford, the famous actor who had recently become senile after directing a civil war movie. –the Narrator.)

Robert snatched his cellphone from Blaine and pointed it at Jesus, pressing the kill button on his app again and again. "Work, damn you! *WORK!*" Robert screamed pointlessly at the phone.

Jesus grabbed the phone. He held it to his face and said, "Haven't you wondered why your phone hasn't come to life during this whole mess and tried to kill you?"

"Because of a major plot hole?" Blaine asked.

"Yeah, and it was also destroyed by that crazy laundry machine-thing," Kevin added.

Jesus sneered at Blaine, and said, "No, you shi—"

Robert punched Jesus square in the jaw, and he went flying against the glass case that housed the kill switch, shattering it. The impact almost knocked the plate of sandwiches over, but Blaine ran over to catch it just in time. And then he and Kevin finally got to eat the delicious sandwiches.

Jesus fell to his knees.

(The author sure likes to get people on their knees a lot, doesn't he? *Hmmmm*... —the Narrator)

Robert stood over him, flexing. He kissed his right bicep, then his left. Then he did lumbar stretches right in front of him. *"Watch this!"* he said, as he did one-handed push-ups. "Bet you wish you could do *that*."

Robert did some sit-ups. Some jumping-jacks. He did so many jumping-jacks it was crazy.

Jesus watched in awe. He actually admired the guy. Robert was in better shape than he himself had ever been in his life. He would never be able to kill this perfect caricature of a man. "I'll never kill you!" Jesus whined, admitting defeat.

Robert got all in his face and was like, an inch away from his nose, making them very close together. "But you said today is the day I *die*, you pudgy fuck of a crazy shit bastard!" Robert sneered.

"Yes. You do," Andrew said, appearing from out of nowhere again. "You're supposed to sacrifice yourself during the last act to save everyone and die a hero."

Robert pondered that thought. Everyone else felt a little relieved, since Andrew could tell the future somehow and knew they were all going to be saved.

"Way to go, Robert!" Blaine said, putting his hand on Robert's shoulder.

"Yeah! I thought we were all going to die down here!" said Amy, hugging the old man.

Kevin looked into his eyes sincerely. "We all love you very much, you know."

Robert smiled, his eyes tearing up a little. Then he looked down at his feet, shuffling them. "Aw, shucks, guys…"

"I love you, too!" said Sean's ghost, lingering above them. But no one heard Sean, so he might as well have still been alive.

"Oh, fuck you guys!" Jesus sneered, like he always did.

Andrew was gone again before anyone could even say anything about him.

Then a little kid (Jimmy) with a knife came running from out of nowhere with a knife and stabbed Jesus in the back. He pulled out the knife and stabbed him again, and again, yelling, "STAB YOU! STAB YOU! STAB YOU! DIE! DIE! DIE!"

Everyone cheered the kid on. Jesus, screaming in pain, fell face-down in a pool of his own blood and died like a lot people in my books always do.

(Really, I couldn't think of anything better. I just wanted Jesus to finally shut up and die at this point. I'm going to go pour a drink to celebrate. I suggest you do the same. —Vince Kramer)

Then the little boy noticed Robert's huge boner and ran away screaming.

"What do we do now?" asked Amy.

Kevin had a flashback and envisioned Andrew floating in his wheelchair, saying *"Kevin-in-in! Start the reactor-or-or! It's the only way to stop Stephen King-ing-ing. From writing a new book ever again-an-an,"* in his weirdo autism voice. "Guys!" Kevin said, "I know what to do! Andrew told me to press that big red button there."

"What does it do?" Amy asked.

113

"I'm pretty sure it's some kind of special kill switch. It will probably turn off all of the machines and end this whole nightmare," he said assuredly.

"Can I do it?" Blaine asked.

"No," Kevin said. "*I* get to do it."

Blaine frowned. "But *I* want to do it!" he said, frowning.

"Well, *too bad...*" Kevin said, and walked gingerly over to the shattered glass case housing the big, red, Stephen King-stopping, world-saving machine-ceasing button.

He pressed it.

There were a bunch of whirring and humming sounds as the big system in the *Missile Command WarGames Room* was obviously doing something cool and tech-related that would be beyond the author to describe.

"Now what?" Robert asked.

"We wait."

About two million missiles hit Russia.

Vladimir Putin was leading an army of Cossacks against the machines. He was shirtless, his muscles glistening with sweat. He brandished his sword, riding a gigantic grizzly bear without a saddle.

(Was he riding it *bearback?* —the Narrator)

Everyone looked up as the missiles streaked across the sky. They exploded in mid-air, raining a cloud of strange dust down on Vladimir and his big army of sexy, muscled men.

Vladimir Putin jumped off his bear and walked up to the closest soldier and stuck his tongue down his throat.

"Oh, Mr. Putin!" he said.

The Russian president looked into his eyes and said, "Please, call me Vlad."

Then he ripped off the soldiers clothes, pulled down his pants, and laid down on top of him—grinding his throbbing manhood against the soldier's as they kissed passionately.

The entire Russian army got completely naked and started sucking each other's dicks and fucking.

It was the most epic gay orgy ever.

Because the big red button didn't do anything but launch Gay Bombs at Russia.

"Well," Kevin said, "I think it's been long enough. Let's get the fuck out of here."

"Up here!" Amy shouted, from a hatch at the top of a ladder she had already found and gone up.

Everyone climbed up the ladder.

And it led straight to the atrium!

Into the Panini Café!

Sandwiches for everybody!

CHAPTER
MRS. COFFEE

"C'mon," Blaine said, chewing on a nice Panini. "Doesn't anyone else want to know what was *really* going on down there?"

"No," Amy said, wiping a spot of mayonnaise off of the corner of her mouth.

"Probably some kind of government conspiracy," Robert said.

"I've never been one to care very much about those," Kevin said. He jumped off the counter in the nice Panini shop and raised his beer. "To Dan, Dave, and all those other people we lost."

(I miss all those guys! Except Sean. —the Narrator)

They all raised their glasses, full of cold beer that they were enjoying.

"You will be remembered," Kevin toasted. "…And when you're remembered, you're never truly lost. Only in our *hearts*."

"Cheers," said Amy.

They all clanged their glasses together.

"Who the hell were all those other people anyway?" Robert asked. "I only remember those cute twin boys that just died."

"Oh," Blaine explained, "There was that retarded guy and that cripple. That bitchy old lady who turned into a cyborg. Some others, I don't remember. I'm more concerned about what was going on in that basement. Not like anyone else cares."

"But," Blaine smiled, "I will tell you one thing. This is one *hell* of a sandwich!"

"Hear, hear!" Kevin cheered.

The atrium was beautiful. Kevin stood at a platform overlooking the massive waterfall and lake as the green sun shone nicely on the meticulous landscape through the dome windows overhead.

He put his arm around Amy, thinking about finally fucking her, maybe. "You know, if Dave were here, he'd probably say that line from *Star Trek II*. The one about the cave in that planet where the scientist chick had turned everything in there all lush and beautiful and plant-like with that Genesis Device."

"I've never seen that movie," Amy said.

"Really? You haven't?" Kevin asked. "Where have you been your whole life? Under a rock?"

"No," she sneered at him. "*OUTER SPACE!*"

Then the nipples on her tits opened up and sprayed hot coffee at him.

Kevin ducked out of the way just in time. He looked up at Amy.

She was a terrifying coffee machine robot. She was black plastic and gray metal. One of her eyes was a blue light, the other green. A red light emanated from her mouth.

Her chest was more impressive than ever, and steaming spouts were now her nipples. Below her breasts, her stomach was a chamber with a pot of freshly brewed coffee inside.

Her right hand had turned into a steel coffee cup, and her left hand, a spoon.

She looked pretty ridiculous.

(Really? I think she looked pretty fucking awesome! — the Narrator)

But she also looked kind of awesome.

And Kevin was in awe of her, so that was probably more accurate. "How long have you been a coffee machine robot?!" he screamed at her. "Like, this whole time?!"

"I have not been Mrs. Coffee for long. But I... I have *always* been. I am limitless, eternal, a *superior roast!*" she said.

"Where's Amy?!" Kevin pleaded. "Amy! You've got to be in there somewhere!"

She disagreed. "Amy is gone now. There is only Mrs. Coffee! There is only *death!*"

Mrs. Coffee grabbed the coffee pot out of her stomach and poured it into her metal coffee cup hand. Hot cream squirted out of her left tit, and she stirred it in with her spoon. Then she offered it to him. "Would you like a freshly brewed cup? Of *oblivion?*"

"NO!!!!!" Kevin screamed.

A drop of the coffee splashed to the ground, where it burned the floor like acid.

"Only the finest, most robust brew of *DEATH.*" She stirred.

The coffee machine woman walked toward him robotically with the cup—no longer Amy, no longer Mimi, and definitely no fucking Mummy. Steaming hot acid-like contents sloshed out of her cup with each step.

Kevin crawled backward on the palms of his hands. "NOOOOO!! Why are you doing this?!"

(Because she's a bitch! Fight her, Kevin! GET UP! Kill the coffee bitch! *KILL HER!* —the Narrator)

"Retaliation. Extermination. *Caffeination!*" she stated— the *real* reasons.

She stood over him. There was nowhere left for Kevin to crawl. Her coffee cup hand began to rotate upside-down, about to spill the contents all over Kevin. He shielded his face with his arms.

The ironic part was that he actually could've gone for a cup of coffee.

Robert and Blaine were passed out on the floor of the Panini Café, wearing nothing but their underwear.

Robert was holding Blaine tightly and they cuddled in a warm embrace. Blaine had rejected all of the old man's sexual advances, but in the end, had let him hold him as he slept. It turned out to be quite comforting and Blaine fell right asleep.

He fantasized about being a child again, and being loved by his grandfather. Being cared about. Having a puppy. It was a warm feeling he lost a long time ago, far buried in the past. And way before all the stuff that happened to Kevin.

Kevin was kidnapped, raped, and molested by a pack of wild cougars. You know, slutty older women that booze a lot and act like dirty truckers.

(Actually, he was just remembering an old dream as if it had really happened. The only really bad thing that happened to Kevin when they were growing up was that he came in second place in a spelling bee, and he's never been able to live it down since. —the Narrator)

Robert dreamed wildly. In his dream, he was invincible. And super-strong. He lifted a tank way over his head and threw it at Abraham Lincoln, where it exploded; killing him everywhere. The president's gigantic spaceship army retreated. He rejoiced, having saved the world, and Lincoln's wife, Mary Todd, got on her knees in front of him and gave him the best blow job he ever had in his life.

He had a nocturnal emission all over Blaine's back.

All of a sudden Blaine started having a nightmare about being trapped in a hundred-story building drowning in cum.

The roller coaster from the hotel lobby sped up the atrium's glass dome, perched on the top, rose its front up like some kind of gigantic death worm and crashed down through the glass. It dove into the big pond in the middle of the atrium in a hail of shattered glass, splashing water and debris everywhere.

The whole spectacle looked like a scene from the 90s film *Anaconda*, starring Jennifer Lopez and Ice Cube, but way more amusing because the roller coaster looked fun and ridiculous and almost not as deadly. It had a happy clown painted on the front. And the red nose lit up.

The rolling death machine rose up out of the water. Mrs. Coffee Amy Cyborg turned to greet it.

Kevin rolled out of the way, behind a bush, where he felt kind of safe for the moment. He watched.

Amy seemed to be communicating with the roller coaster. It blinked its headlights in a wild fashion that seemed to denote it was talking to her in Morse Code.

And for the first time, Kevin looked through the big hole in the dome and noticed that the sky was no longer green, but blue. Like normal. Maybe starting the reactor *had* done something.

(Something beside turning Russia gay? —the Narrator)

"HOLY SHIT!" Blaine screamed when the roller coaster shattered the glass dome. They were out of sight but the sound was so loud that it obviously meant nothing good was going on.

Robert put his hand over Blaine's mouth immediately and told him to shush, knowing Blaine's loud blathering would reveal their location to whatever hellish death machine lurked out there.

Then Blaine felt the wetness on his back, and immediately knew what it was. "DID YOU FUCKING RAPE ME IN MY SLEEP OLD MAN!?" he yelled.

Robert then noticed what had happened, and got a little

embarrassed. "Sorry son, must've had a wet dream. But no raping went on, I swear it." Robert heard mechanical noises coming from outside, loud ones, getting closer. "And now they're coming to get us! You've really done it now, son!" he yelled at Blaine.

"Sorry!" Blaine whispered. "What do we do?"

Robert grabbed him tight, shielding him with his body. He whispered in his ear, "Hold on for dear life. This is going to hurt."

The roller coaster burst through the roof of the café and snaked around the place destroying everything in its path. It exploded in a fury of wood, glass, metal, and sandwiches.

(Were they death sandwiches now? Death sandwiches of DEATH, maybe? Hey, that should be the title of Stephen King's next book. —the Narrator)

Mrs. Coffee found Kevin again, and poured him another cup of coffee. "No one escapes Mrs. Coffee. Nothing escapes *death*." She pointed at the roller coaster emerging from the rubble behind him. "Prepare yourself," she said. "You're going for a ride."

Kevin panicked. He didn't know which was worse, being burned to death by hot coffee or being crushed to death by a killer roller coaster. He felt like he was in the middle of a death sandwich, and would be killed by both. He felt like nothing but a piece of meat.

But when he turned to see the big killing thing on wheels coming at him, snakelike, he was pleasantly surprised to see his brother and Robert in the front seat, riding it.

"Get out of the way!" Robert screamed to Kevin.

Kevin rolled out of the way as quickly as he could,

scraping his knees on the ground, which hurt really bad.

Robert jumped out of the front seat, launching straight at Amy like a human cannonball. "NYEEEEEARGH!" he screamed like a battle cry.

(That's my favorite expression. Not, "battle cry"— *"NYEEEEEARGH!"* —the Narrator)

He knocked into her so hard that the coffee pot in her stomach chamber shattered. Robert screamed in pain as the liquid acid sprayed all over him, burning him severely.

The Mrs. Coffee robot stumbled backward, losing her balance, and fell on her back.

Robert screamed his battle cry again, (*"NYEEEEEARGH!"*), and stomped and stomped on her face and chest. She broke and cracked in places, hot steam escaping from her wounds, which also burned Robert. But he didn't stop. He kept stomping and stomping until blood started pouring out of her as well. And he didn't stop there either. He kept at it until her metal casings were completely caved in, and guts and brains started spilling out.

When he finally stopped, she lay twitching and sparking and bleeding and dying. She let out a death rattle, which went *"SCREEEEEEEE!"* and changed to, *"101010110110101010101!!!!"* Whatever that sounds like.

Robert collapsed into Kevin's arms.

"I got you, Robert!" Kevin said.

Robert looked up at him. "I did it Kevin, I saved you, and I saved your brother. And I finally killed that cunt, Amy."

Kevin teared up. "Yes, Robert. Yes, you did. You saved the day! You *saved us.* I *knew* you could do it!"

Robert coughed up some blood. It smelled like whiskey. "I hope I've made you proud, son. Now I can finally rest in peace. And please, just promise me something…"

Kevin wiped a tear from his cheek. "What's that, Robert?"

"Keep on living. Not in fear, but in hope. Don't treat every day like it's your last, but treat every day like it's your *first*. The world is yours. Never let it get you down. These machines aren't going to last forever. Hell, they'll probably even run out of gas or batteries or whatever else is powering them. Then it will be a new day, Kevin," Robert choked on some tears, "a *new day*. Make me proud, son."

Kevin cried, "I will, Robert! I'll live. *Live!*"

"Live. Make me proud!"

"You'll be the *proudest*. I love you, Robert."

"*New day...*" Robert sputtered. And then he slumped in Kevin's arms and died.

Kevin screamed, "*NOOOOOOOOOOOO!!!!*"

And then Robert farted and shit himself. It reeked.

"*EWWWWWWWWW!!!!*" Kevin yelled, and quickly let go of Robert's corpse, pushing it off of him. Then he stood up and accidentally puked all over it.

"Uh, a little help up here?"

Kevin wiped the tears from his face and turned to see Blaine, still sitting in the front seat of the roller coaster, which appeared to be frozen in place.

"What happened to it?" Kevin shouted up at him.

"I don't know, it just... *stopped*."

"Hold on, I'll climb up the back of it so I can reach you."

When Kevin got to the front seat where Blaine was, he recoiled in horror. The safety bar had gone completely through Blaine's body. It had squished right through the middle of him, and was holding his torso up in the seat.

He looked at his brother, who seemed to be unaware of what had happened. "Oh no, not you, too, Blaine..."

"What? What's wrong?"

"You've... you've been crushed by the safety bar. Can't you see it?"

"No... I think my back is broken. I can't feel anything."

"You're paralyzed. And I think the bar is the only thing keeping you alive. If I try to pull it off of you," Kevin sniffled, "you'll *die!*"

"Well, we all gotta die sometime."

"NO! Not you, Blaine! NOT *YOU!*"

"Kevin, look. There's no time for this. I think I know why the roller coaster stopped. I can feel it making little machine noises again. I think it's getting a message from the other machines. It's going to take off at any moment and probably kill you. You've got to get out of here."

"Not without you!"

"Yes, yes without me. I'm sorry, Kevin. I'm sorry I let you down."

"But it's supposed to be a *new day!*"

"Yes, yes. I heard the whole speech. Look, I'm going to die here one way or another. You have to go. You have to do everything Robert told you to. This is goodbye from me as well."

Kevin wiped the tears from his face. "Okay, I guess I have no choice. Goodbye, Blaine."

"Oh, and Kevin? Can you pretend that I just said everything Robert said to you before he died?"

"Sure. The old man had a way with words, didn't he?"

"Yeah. He sure did. Anyways, I'm going to die now. Get the fuck out here."

Kevin climbed down the machine and tried to find an escape route. The roller coaster came back to life and snaked out of the atrium, back up through the ceiling.

"Goodbye, Blaine," Kevin said as he watched the coiling machine take off with his brother's lonely corpse.

124

FINAL CHAPTER

"I'm all alone now," Kevin said to himself. "They're all dead."

Then a modestly-sized UFO came through the hole in the dome and shot lasers at the gigantic death coaster. It exploded.

"HOLY SHIT!" Kevin screamed.

The UFO flew right up to Kevin and stalled. The hatch opened and a figure was visible inside the unidentified object that wasn't flying anymore and so was just a UO. "Forget about me?" asked Andrew, victoriously from the cockpit of the shiny craft.

Kevin was absolutely surprised. "Actually, yeah. Yeah I did. Um… sorry."

"No worries. Now, hop in."

Kevin climbed up the side of the ship and got inside with Andrew.

"You ready?" the autistic kid asked.

"Ready as I'll ever be, I guess."

"Good. I have a lot to tell you. A lot to *show you*. Let's go."

The UFO went back up through the atrium window and flew out of the Grand Ole Gay Times Opryland Resort and Convention Center once and for all.

Kevin surveyed the widespread paths of destruction beneath him. "The world…"

"Yes. It has mostly been destroyed," Andrew said.

"What happened?"

"Have a space beer." Andrew handed him an ice cold brew covered in strange alien markings. The label had a Grey alien with big black eyes wearing a cowboy hat pretending to shoot guns at you. It *definitely* looked like something Kevin wanted to drink.

Kevin accepted it, but still gave the kid a kind-of dirty look. He drank the space beer. It was the best beer he ever had in his life. "Jesus! This is the best beer I've ever had in my life."

"I'm Andrew. Jesus is dead now, remember?" Andrew smiled at him.

Kevin remembered, slamming his beer. "Okay, now tell me what the hell just happened to the Earth," he said.

Andrew put his hand over Kevin's, and said, "Open your mind…"

All of Andrew's knowledge poured into him.

Kevin puked. He hoped Andrew had more space beer because he'd just made him waste one.

"You have always had eyes but you have been blind. Now you can see. What do you see, Kevin?" Andrew asked.

"So many… *alternate endings*," Kevin said dreamily.

"There can be only one."

"Hey! That was Dave's line!" Kevin shouted. He was sure that the autistic kid was way too young to know that movie.

Andrew said, "I assure you, I'm quite familiar with the *Highlander* franchise." Because he could read Kevin's mind.

Kevin looked at him, stupefied. "There's only one way this is ending, isn't it?"

"Yes. And it isn't the ending where you get to go to McDonald's."

That was disappointing. Kevin loved McDonald's. But, he went with the one scenario that Andrew was obviously talking about. It's explained in the FINAL final chapter.

FINAL FINAL CHAPTER

The comet was sent by a malevolent alien force from deep space, to sweep Earth clean of life.

It brought all the planet's machines to life to do the dirty work, using cosmic rays and lost souls of the alien dead. They were then going to come to Earth and populate it. They had gotten the idea from countless Earth movies and books where the same exact thing happened.

They succeeded. In part. But they weren't counting on one thing—an opposing alien race that loved Earth and stood against them. The good aliens had been visiting the planet for years as tourists, and sometimes, secret friends.

They mapped the world and always came to take photographs of their favorite monuments and landscapes. Their people had their favorite spots on the planet and often couldn't wait to show their friends.

And they loved humans because they were ridiculous and fun—they made great movies, great music, wrote great books, and were mostly good and kind or at least amusing, even the nasty perverted ones who fucked retards in the mouth.

Sometimes the aliens would pick a human up in a spaceship and take them on an awesome space adventure, just to show them how much they cared.

And they cared. Oh, how they cared. They might've been a little late, but they had commandeered a machine planet that had been abandoned by the malevolent alien villains that came to destroy all life on Earth. They teleported as many humans as they could to it, saving many lives. They used a human conduit to put a stop to the machines that

128

were destroying the Earthlings. It had to be someone with an ability (which sadly was considered a *dis*ability on Earth) that would be able to understand the Universal Language, and wield the gift of uber-mega technology.

A young autistic boy had first understood, and was given the full power and understanding. It was one of the greatest gifts they had ever given to such a member of humanity.

Andrew had done much in a short time. But time was running short for him. He needed to take his medication, count the threads in his favorite blanket, and read a picture book. It was up to the other now. Earth's last hope:

Kevin.

EPILOGUE CHAPTER

The spaceship left Kevin on a mountain peak in Sedona, Arizona.

The machines, now sluggish, slowly crawled over the vacant world, wreaking havoc and destruction on all that remained. Their weakened threat was *still...* a THREAT.

Andrew's craft went to rejoin the others on the machine planet, leaving Kevin as the last inhabitant of Earth. They would return in twenty-two years. Until then, the Earth was his. The power. The knowing. The *new day*. All of it was Kevin's.

Kevin stood high on his mountain and looked down at the valley below him. The machines appeared to be so small from there. Like ants. Or stupid bugs that were even dumber than ants. Like they were *nothing*. Kevin glowed with power. An extra-terrestrial cosmic force thrilled every fiber of his frame. He clenched his fists—it was *go time*.

He looked down at the valley of the death machines of death, and let out his battle cry. *"CATCHPHRASE!"*

BIZARRO AUTHOR
VINCE KRAMER
FUNCTION:
LEADER

"Peace through tyranny!"

VINCE is a combination of brute strength, military cunning, ruthlessness and terror. He aches to return to Cybertron to complete his conquest after destroying all the machines on Earth and capturing all Earth resources. He's incredibly powerful and intelligent and fires a nuclear charged fusion cannon. He can also link up interdimensionally to a black hole and draw anti-matter from it for use as a weapon.

Vince has no known weaknesses.

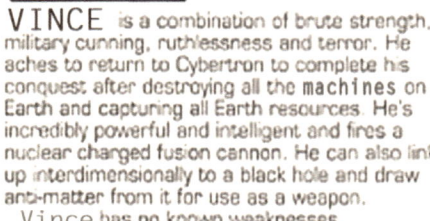

	1	2	3	4	5	6	7	8	9	10
STRENGTH										
INTELLIGENCE										
SPEED										
ENDURANCE										
RANK										
COURAGE										
FIREPOWER										
SKILL										

BIZARRO BOOKS

CATALOG   SPRING 2013

ERASERHEAD PRESS

Your major resource for the bizarro fiction genre:

WWW.BIZARROCENTRAL.COM

Introduce yourselves to the bizarro fiction genre and all of its authors with the Bizarro Starter Kit series. Each volume features short novels and short stories by ten of the leading bizarro authors, designed to give you a perfect sampling of the genre for only $10.

BB-0X1
"The Bizarro Starter Kit" (Orange)
Featuring D. Harlan Wilson, Carlton Mellick III, Jeremy Robert Johnson, Kevin L Donihe, Gina Ranalli, Andre Duza, Vincent W. Sakowski, Steve Beard, John Edward Lawson, and Bruce Taylor. **236 pages $10**

BB-0X2
"The Bizarro Starter Kit" (Blue)
Featuring Ray Fracalossy, Jeremy C. Shipp, Jordan Krall, Mykle Hansen, Andersen Prunty, Eckhard Gerdes, Bradley Sands, Steve Aylett, Christian TeBordo, and Tony Rauch. **244 pages $10**

BB-0X2
"The Bizarro Starter Kit" (Purple)
Featuring Russell Edson, Athena Villaverde, David Agranoff, Matthew Revert, Andrew Goldfarb, Jeff Burk, Garrett Cook, Kris Saknussemm, Cody Goodfellow, and Cameron Pierce **264 pages $10**

BB-001"**The Kafka Effekt" D. Harlan Wilson** — A collection of forty-four irreal short stories loosely written in the vein of Franz Kafka, with more than a pinch of William S. Burroughs sprinkled on top. **211 pages $14**

BB-002 **"Satan Burger" Carlton Mellick III** — The cult novel that put Carlton Mellick III on the map ... Six punks get jobs at a fast food restaurant owned by the devil in a city violently overpopulated by surreal alien cultures. **236 pages $14**

BB-003 **"Some Things Are Better Left Unplugged" Vincent Sakwoski** — Join The Man and his Nemesis, the obese tabby, for a nightmare roller coaster ride into this postmodern fantasy. **152 pages $10**

BB-005 **"Razor Wire Pubic Hair" Carlton Mellick III** — A genderless humandildo is purchased by a razor dominatrix and brought into her nightmarish world of bizarre sex and mutilation. **176 pages $11**

BB-007 **"The Baby Jesus Butt Plug" Carlton Mellick III** — Using clones of the Baby Jesus for anal sex will be the hip sex fetish of the future. **92 pages $10**

BB-010 **"The Menstruating Mall" Carlton Mellick III** — "The Breakfast Club meets Chopping Mall as directed by David Lynch." - Brian Keene **212 pages $12**

BB-011 **"Angel Dust Apocalypse" Jeremy Robert Johnson** — Meth-heads, man-made monsters, and murderous Neo-Nazis. "Seriously amazing short stories..." - Chuck Palahniuk, author of Fight Club **184 pages $11**

BB-015 **"Foop!" Chris Genoa** — Strange happenings are going on at Dactyl. Inc, the world's first and only time travel tourism company.
"A surreal pie in the face!" - Christopher Moore **300 pages $14**

BB-032 **"Extinction Journals" Jeremy Robert Johnson** — An uncanny voyage across a newly nuclear America where one man must confront the problems associated with loneliness, insane dieties, radiation, love, and an ever-evolving cockroach suit with a mind of its own. **104 pages $10**

BB-037 **"The Haunted Vagina" Carlton Mellick III** — It's difficult to love a woman whose vagina is a gateway to the world of the dead. **132 pages $10**

BB-043 **"War Slut" Carlton Mellick III** — Part "1984," part "Waiting for Godot," and part action horror video game adaptation of John Carpenter's "The Thing." **116 pages $10**

BB-047 **"Sausagey Santa" Carlton Mellick III** — A bizarro Christmas tale featuring Santa as a piratey mutant with a body made of sausages. 124 pages $10

BB-048 **"Misadventures in a Thumbnail Universe" Vincent Sakowski** — Dive deep into the surreal and satirical realms of neo-classical Blender Fiction, filled with television shoes and flesh-filled skies. **120 pages $10**

BB-053 **"Ballad of a Slow Poisoner" Andrew Goldfarb** — Millford Mutterwurst sat down on a Tuesday to take his afternoon tea, and made the unpleasant discovery that his elbows were becoming flatter. **128 pages $10**

BB-055 **"Help! A Bear is Eating Me" Mykle Hansen** — The bizarro, heartwarming, magical tale of poor planning, hubris and severe blood loss... **150 pages $11**

BB-056 **"Piecemeal June" Jordan Krall** — A man falls in love with a living sex doll, but with love comes danger when her creator comes after her with crab-squid assassins. **90 pages $9**

BB-058 **"The Overwhelming Urge" Andersen Prunty** — A collection of bizarro tales by Andersen Prunty. **150 pages** **$11**

BB-059 **"Adolf in Wonderland" Carlton Mellick III** — A dreamlike adventure that takes a young descendant of Adolf Hitler's design and sends him down the rabbit hole into a world of imperfection and disorder. **180 pages** **$11**

BB-061 **"Ultra Fuckers" Carlton Mellick III** — Absurdist suburban horror about a couple who enter an upper middle class gated community but can't find their way out. **108 pages** **$9**

BB-062 **"House of Houses" Kevin L. Donihe** — An odd man wants to marry his house. Unfortunately, all of the houses in the world collapse at the same time in the Great House Holocaust. Now he must travel to House Heaven to find his departed fiancee. **172 pages** **$11**

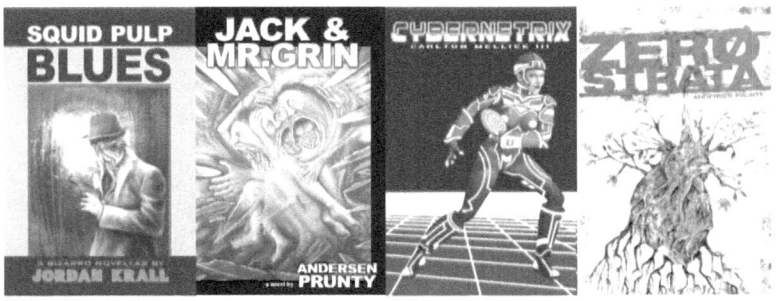

BB-064 **"Squid Pulp Blues" Jordan Krall** — In these three bizarro-noir novellas, the reader is thrown into a world of murderers, drugs made from squid parts, deformed gun-toting veterans, and a mischievous apocalyptic donkey. **204 pages $12**

BB-065 **"Jack and Mr. Grin" Andersen Prunty** — "When Mr. Grin calls you can hear a smile in his voice. Not a warm and friendly smile, but the kind that seizes your spine in fear. You don't need to pay your phone bill to hear it. That smile is in every line of Prunty's prose." - Tom Bradley. **208 pages** **$12**

BB-066 **"Cybernetrix" Carlton Mellick III** — What would you do if your normal everyday world was slowly mutating into the video game world from Tron? **212 pages** **$12**

BB-072 **"Zerostrata" Andersen Prunty** — Hansel Nothing lives in a tree house, suffers from memory loss, has a very eccentric family, and falls in love with a woman who runs naked through the woods every night. **144 pages $11**

BB-073 **"The Egg Man" Carlton Mellick III** — It is a world where humans reproduce like insects. Children are the property of corporations, and having an enormous ten-foot brain implanted into your skull is a grotesque sexual fetish. Mellick's industrial urban dystopia is one of his darkest and grittiest to date. **184 pages** **$11**

BB-074 **"Shark Hunting in Paradise Garden" Cameron Pierce** — A group of strange humanoid religious fanatics travel back in time to the Garden of Eden to discover it is invested with hundreds of giant flying maneating sharks. **150 pages** **$10**

BB-075 **"Apeshit" Carlton Mellick III** - Friday the 13th meets Visitor Q. Six hipster teens go to a cabin in the woods inhabited by a deformed killer. An incredibly fucked-up parody of B-horror movies with a bizarro slant. **192 pages** **$12**

BB-076 **"Fuckers of Everything on the Crazy Shitting Planet of the Vomit At smosphere" Mykle Hansen** - Three bizarro satires. Monster Cocks, Journey to the Center of Agnes Cuddlebottom, and Crazy Shitting Planet. **228 pages** **$12**

BB-077 **"The Kissing Bug" Daniel Scott Buck** — In the tradition of Roald Dahl, Tim Burton, and Edward Gorey, comes this bizarro anti-war children's story about a bohemian conenose kissing bug who falls in love with a human woman. **116 pages** **$10**

BB-078 **"MachoPoni" Lotus Rose** — It's My Little Pony... *Bizarro* style! A long time ago Poniworld was split in two. On one side of the Jagged Line is the Pastel Kingdom, a magical land of music, parties, and positivity. On the other side of the Jagged Line is Dark Kingdom inhabited by an army of undead ponies. **148 pages** **$11**

BB-079 **"The Faggiest Vampire" Carlton Mellick III** — A Roald Dahl-esque children's story about two faggy vampires who partake in a mustache competition to find out which one is truly the faggiest. **104 pages $10**

BB-080 **"Sky Tongues" Gina Ranalli** — The autobiography of Sky Tongues, the biracial hermaphrodite actress with tongues for fingers. Follow her strange life story as she rises from freak to fame. **204 pages $12**

BB-081 **"Washer Mouth" Kevin L. Donihe** - A washing machine becomes human and pursues his dream of meeting his favorite soap opera star. **244 pages $11**

BB-082 **"Shatnerquake" Jeff Burk** - All of the characters ever played by William Shatner are suddenly sucked into our world. Their mission: hunt down and destroy the real William Shatner. **100 pages $10**

BB-083 **"The Cannibals of Candyland" Carlton Mellick III** - There exists a race of cannibals that are made of candy. They live in an underground world made out of candy. One man has dedicated his life to killing them all. **170 pages $11**

BB-084 **"Slub Glub in the Weird World of the Weeping Willows" Andrew Goldfarb** - The charming tale of a blue glob named Slub Glub who helps the weeping willows whose tears are flooding the earth. There are also hyeras, ghosts, and a voodoo priest **100 pages $10**

BB-085 **"Super Fetus" Adam Pepper** - Try to abort this fetus and he'll kick your ass! **104 pages $10**

BB-086 **"Fistful of Feet" Jordan Krall** - A bizarro tribute to spaghetti westerns, featuring Cthulhu-worshipping Indians, a woman with four feet, a crazed gunman who is obsessed with sucking on candy, Syphilis-ridden mutants, sexually transmitted tattoos, and a house devoted to the freakiest fetishes. **228 pages $12**

BB-087 **"Ass Goblins of Auschwitz" Cameron Pierce** - It's Monty Python meets Nazi exploitation in a surreal nightmare as can only be imagined by Bizarro author Cameron Pierce. **104 pages $10**

BB-088 **"Silent Weapons for Quiet Wars" Cody Goodfellow** - "This is high-end psychological surrealist horror meets bottom-feeding low-life crime in a techno-thrilling science fiction world full of Lovecraft and magic..." -John Skipp **212 pages $12**

BB-089 "Warrior Wolf Women of the Wasteland" Carlton Mellick III
— Road Warrior Werewolves versus McDonaldland Mutants...post-apocalyptic fiction has never been quite like this. **316 pages $13**

BB-091 "Super Giant Monster Time" Jeff Burk — A tribute to choose your own adventures and Godzilla movies. Will you escape the giant monsters that are rampaging the fuck out of your city and shit? Or will you join the mob of alien-controlled punk rockers causing chaos in the streets? What happens next depends on you. **188 pages $12**

BB-092 "Perfect Union" Cody Goodfellow — "Cronenberg's THE FLY on a grand scale: human/insect gene-spliced body horror, where the human hive politics are as shocking as the gore." -John Skipp. **272 pages $13**

BB-093 "Sunset with a Beard" Carlton Mellick III — 14 stories of surreal science fiction. **200 pages $12**

BB-094 "My Fake War" Andersen Prunty — The absurd tale of an unlikely soldier forced to fight a war that, quite possibly, does not exist. It's Rambo meets Waiting for Godot in this subversive satire of American values and the scope of the human imagination. **128 pages $11**

BB-095 "Lost in Cat Brain Land" Cameron Pierce — Sad stories from a surreal world. A fascist mustache, the ghost of Franz Kafka, a desert inside a dead cat. Primordial entities mourn the death of their child. The desperate serve tea to mysterious creatures. A hopeless romantic falls in love with a pterodactyl. And much more. **152 pages $11**

BB-096 "The Kobold Wizard's Dildo of Enlightenment +2" Carlton Mellick III — A Dungeons and Dragons parody about a group of people who learn they are only made up characters in an AD&D campaign and must find a way to resist their nerdy teenaged players and retarded dungeon master in order to survive. 232 **pages $12**

BB-098 "A Hundred Horrible Sorrows of Ogner Stump" Andrew Goldfarb — Goldfarb's acclaimed comic series. A magical and weird journey into the horrors of everyday life. **164 pages $11**

BB-099 **"Pickled Apocalypse of Pancake Island" Cameron Pierce**—A demented fairy tale about a pickle, a pancake, and the apocalypse. **102 pages $8**

BB-100 **"Slag Attack" Andersen Prunty**— Slag Attack features four visceral, noir stories about the living, crawling apocalypse.A slag is what survivors are calling the slug-like maggots raining from the sky, burrowing inside people, and hollowing out their flesh and their sanity. **148 pages $11**

BB-101 **"Slaughterhouse High" Robert Devereaux**—A place where schools are built with secret passageways, rebellious teens get zippers installed in their mouths and genitals, and once a year, on that special night, one couple is slaughtered and the bits of their bodies are kept as souvenirs. **304 pages $13**

BB-102 **"The Emerald Burrito of Oz" John Skipp & Marc Levinthal** —OZ IS REAL! Magic is real! The gate is really in Kansas! And America is finally allowing Earth tourists to visit this weird-ass, mysterious land. But when Gene of Los Angeles heads off for summer vacation in the Emerald City, little does he know that a war is brewing...a war that could destroy both worlds. **280 pages $13**

BB-103 **"The Vegan Revolution... with Zombies" David Agranoff** — When there's no more meat in hell, the vegans will walk the earth. **160 pages $11**

BB-104 **"The Flappy Parts" Kevin L Donihe**—Poems about bunnies, LSD, and police abuse. You know, things that matter. **132 pages $11**

BB-105 **"Sorry I Ruined Your Orgy" Bradley Sands**—Bizarro humorist Bradley Sands returns with one of the strangest, most hilarious collections of the year. **130 pages $11**

BB-106 **"Mr. Magic Realism" Bruce Taylor**—Like Golden Age science fiction comics written by Freud, *Mr. Magic Realism* is a strange, insightful adventure that spans the furthest reaches of the galaxy, exploring the hidden caverns in the hearts and minds of men, women, aliens, and biomechanical cats. **152 pages $11**

BB-107 "Zombies and Shit" Carlton Mellick III—"Battle Royale" meets "Return of the Living Dead." Mellick's bizarro tribute to the zombie genre. **308 pages $13**

BB-108 "The Cannibal's Guide to Ethical Living" Mykle Hansen—Over a five star French meal of fine wine, organic vegetables and human flesh, a lunatic delivers a witty, chilling, disturbingly sane argument in favor of eating the rich.. **184 pages $11**

BB-109 "Starfish Girl" Athena Villaverde—In a post-apocalyptic underwater dome society, a girl with a starfish growing from her head and an assassin with sea anenome hair are on the run from a gang of mutant fish men. **160 pages $11**

BB-110 "Lick Your Neighbor" Chris Genoa—Mutant ninjas, a talking whale, kung fu masters, maniacal pilgrims, and an alcoholic clown populate Chris Genoa's surreal, darkly comical and unnerving reimagining of the first Thanksgiving. **303 pages $13**

BB-111 "Night of the Assholes" Kevin L. Donihe—A plague of assholes is infecting the countryside. Normal everyday people are transforming into jerks, snobs, dicks, and douchebags. And they all have only one purpose: to make your life a living hell.. **192 pages $11**

BB-112 "Jimmy Plush, Teddy Bear Detective" Garrett Cook—Hard-boiled cases of a private detective trapped within a teddy bear body. **180 pages $11**

BB-113 "The Deadheart Shelters" Forrest Armstrong—The hip hop lovechild of William Burroughs and Dali... **144 pages $11**

BB-114 "Eyeballs Growing All Over Me... Again" Tony Raugh—Absurd, surreal, playful, dream-like, whimsical, and a lot of fun to read. **144 pages $11**

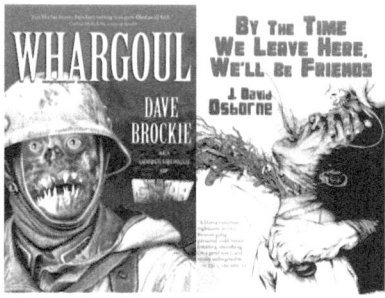  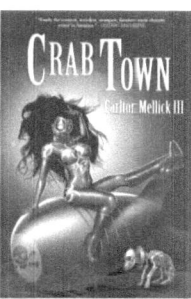

BB-115 **"Whargoul" Dave Brockie** — From the killing grounds of Stalingrad to the death camps of the holocaust. From torture chambers in Iraq to race riots in the United States, the Whargoul was there, killing and raping. **244 pages $12**

BB-116 **"By the Time We Leave Here, We'll Be Friends" J. David Osborne** — A David Lynchian nightmare set in a Russian gulag, where its prisoners, guards, traitors, soldiers, lovers, and demons fight for survival and their own rapidly deteriorating humanity. **168 pages $11**

BB-117 **"Christmas on Crack" edited by Carlton Mellick III** — Perverted Christmas Tales for the whole family! . . . as long as every member of your family is over the age of 18. **168 pages $11**

BB-118 **"Crab Town" Carlton Mellick III** — Radiation fetishists, balloon people, mutant crabs, sail-bike road warriors, and a love affair between a woman and an H-Bomb. This is one mean asshole of a city. Welcome to Crab Town. **100 pages $8**

  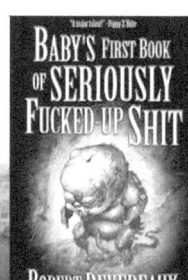 

BB-119 **"Rico Slade Will Fucking Kill You" Bradley Sands** — Rico Slade is an action hero. Rico Slade can rip out a throat with his bare hands. Rico Slade's favorite food is the honey-roasted peanut. Rico Slade will fucking kill everyone. A novel. **122 pages $8**

BB-120 **"Sinister Miniatures" Kris Saknussemm** — The definitive collection of short fiction by Kris Saknussemm, confirming that he is one of the best, most daring writers of the weird to emerge in the twenty-first century. **180 pages $11**

BB-121 **"Baby's First Book of Seriously Fucked up Shit" Robert Devereaux** — Ten stories of the strange, the gross, and the just plain fucked up from one of the most original voices in horror. **176 pages $11**

BB-122 **"The Morbidly Obese Ninja" Carlton Mellick III** — These days, if you want to run a successful company . . . you're going to need a lot of ninjas. **92 pages $8**

BB-123 **"Abortion Arcade" Cameron Pierce** — An intoxicating blend of body horror and midnight movie madness, reminiscent of early David Lynch and the splatterpunks at their most sublime. **172 pages $11**

BB-124 **"Black Hole Blues" Patrick Wensink** — A hilarious double helix of country music and physics. **196 pages $11**

BB-125 **"Barbarian Beast Bitches of the Badlands" Carlton Mellick III** — Three prequels and sequels to *Warrior Wolf Women of the Wasteland.* **284 pages $13**

BB-126 **"The Traveling Dildo Salesman" Kevin L. Donihe** — A nightmare comedy about destiny, faith, and sex toys. Also featuring Donihe's most lurid and infamous short stories: *Milky Agitation, Two-Way Santa, The Helen Mower, Living Room Zombies,* and *Revenge of the Living Masturbation Rag.* **108 pages $8**

BB-127 **"Metamorphosis Blues" Bruce Taylor** — Enter a land of love beasts, intergalactic cowboys, and rock 'n roll. A land where Sears Catalogs are doorways to insanity and men keep mysterious black boxes. Welcome to the monstrous mind of Mr. Magic Realism. **136 pages $11**

BB-128 **"The Driver's Guide to Hitting Pedestrians" Andersen Prunty** — A pocket guide to the twenty-three most painful things in life, written by the most well-adjusted man in the universe. **108 pages $8**

BB-129 **"Island of the Super People" Kevin Shamel** — Four students and their anthropology professor journey to a remote island to study its indigenous population. But this is no ordinary native culture. They're super heroes and villains with flesh costumes and outlandish abilities like self-detonation, musical eyelashes, and microwave hands. **194 pages $11**

BB-130 **"Fantastic Orgy" Carlton Mellick III** — Shark Sex, mutant cats, and strange sexually transmitted diseases. Featuring the stories: *Candy-coated, Ear Cat, Fantastic Orgy, City Hobgoblins,* and *Porno in August.* **136 pages $9**

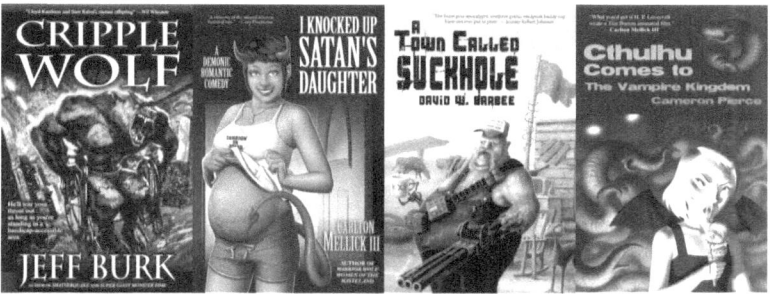

BB-131 "Cripple Wolf" Jeff Burk — Part man. Part wolf. 100% crippled. Also including *Punk Rock Nursing Home, Adrift with Space Badgers, Cook for Your Life, Just Another Day in the Park, Frosty and the Full Monty,* and *House of Cats.* **152 pages $10**

BB-132 "I Knocked Up Satan's Daughter" Carlton Mellick III — An adorable, violent, fantastical love story. A romantic comedy for the bizarro fiction reader. **152 pages $10**

BB-133 "A Town Called Suckhole" David W. Barbee — Far into the future, in the nuclear bowels of post-apocalyptic Dixie, there is a town. A town of derelict mobile homes, ancient junk, and mutant wildlife. A town of slack jawed rednecks who bask in the splendors of moonshine and mud boggin'. A town dedicated to the bloody and demented legacy of the Old South. A town called Suckhole. **144 pages $10**

BB-134 "Cthulhu Comes to the Vampire Kingdom" Cameron Pierce — What you'd get if H. P. Lovecraft wrote a Tim Burton animated film. **148 pages $11**

BB-135 "I am Genghis Cum" Violet LeVoit — From the savage Arctic tundra to post-partum mutations to your missing daughter's unmarked grave, join visionary madwoman Violet LeVoit in this non-stop eight-story onslaught of full-tilt Bizarro punk lit thrills. **124 pages $9**

BB-136 "Haunt" Laura Lee Bahr — A tripping-balls Los Angeles noir, where a mysterious dame drags you through a time-warping Bizarro hall of mirrors. **316 pages $13**

BB-137 "Amazing Stories of the Flying Spaghetti Monster" edited by Cameron Pierce — Like an all-spaghetti evening of Adult Swim, the Flying Spaghetti Monster will show you the many realms of His Noodly Appendage. Learn of those who worship him and the lives he touches in distant, mysterious ways. **228 pages $12**

BB-138 "Wave of Mutilation" Douglas Lain — A dream-pop exploration of modern architecture and the American identity, *Wave of Mutilation* is a Zen finger trap for the 21st century. **100 pages $8**

BB-139 **"Hooray for Death!" Mykle Hansen** — Famous Author Mykle Hansen draws unconventional humor from deaths tiny and large, and invites you to laugh while you can. **128 pages $10**

BB-140 **"Hypno-hog's Moonshine Monster Jamboree" Andrew Goldfarb** — Hicks, Hogs, Horror! Goldfarb is back with another strange illustrated tale of backwoods weirdness. **120 pages $9**

BB-141 **"Broken Piano For President" Patrick Wensink** — A comic masterpiece about the fast food industry, booze, and the necessity to choose happiness over work and security. **372 pages $15**

BB-142 **"Please Do Not Shoot Me in the Face" Bradley Sands** — A novel in three parts, *Please Do Not Shoot Me in the Face: A Novel*, is the story of one boy detective, the worst ninja in the world, and the great American fast food wars. It is a novel of loss, destruction, and--incredibly--genuine hope. **224 pages $12**

BB-143 **"Santa Steps Out" Robert Devereaux** — Sex, Death, and Santa Claus ... The ultimate erotic Christmas story is back. **294 pages $13**

BB-144 **"Santa Conquers the Homophobes" Robert Devereaux** — "I wish I could hope to ever attain one-thousandth the perversity of Robert Devereaux's toenail clippings." - Poppy Z. Brite **316 pages $13**

BB-145 **"We Live Inside You" Jeremy Robert Johnson** — "Jeremy Robert Johnson is dancing to a way different drummer. He loves language, he loves the edge, and he loves us people. These stories have range and style and wit. This is entertainment... and literature."- Jack Ketchum **188 pages $11**

BB-146 **"Clockwork Girl" Athena Villaverde** — Urban fairy tales for the weird girl in all of us. Like a combination of Francesca Lia Block, Charles de Lint, Kathe Koja, Tim Burton, and Hayao Miyazaki, her stories are cute, kinky, edgy, magical, provocative, and strange, full of poetic imagery and vicious sexuality. **160 pages $10**

BB-147 **"Armadillo Fists" Carlton Mellick III** — A weird-as-hell gangster story set in a world where people drive giant mechanical dinosaurs instead of cars **168 pages $11**

BB-148 **"Gargoyle Girls of Spider Island" Cameron Pierce** — Four college seniors venture out into open waters for the tropical party weekend of a lifetime. Instead of a teenage sex fantasy, they find themselves in a nightmare of pirates, sharks, and sex-crazed monsters. **100 pages $8**

BB-149 **"The Handsome Squirm" by Carlton Mellick III** — Like Franz Kafka's *The Trial* meets an erotic body horror version of *The Blob*. **158 pages $11**

BB-150 **"Tentacle Death Trip" Jordan Krall** — It's *Death Race 2000* meets H. P. Lovecraft in bizarro author Jordan Krall's best and most suspenseful work to date. **224 pages $12**

BB-151 **"The Obese" Nick Antosca** — Like Alfred Hitchcock's *The Birds*... but with obese people. **108 pages $10**

BB-152 **"All-Monster Action!" Cody Goodfellow** — The world gave him a blank check and a demand: Create giant monsters to fight our wars. But Dr. Otaku was not satisfied with mere chaos and mass destruction.... **216 pages $12**

BB-153 **"Ugly Heaven" Carlton Mellick III** — Heaven is no longer a paradise. It was once a blissful utopia full of wonders far beyond human comprehension. But the afterlife is now in ruins. It has become an ugly, lonely wasteland populated by strange monstrous beasts, masturbating angels, and sad man-like beings wallowing in the remains of the once-great Kingdom of God. **106 pages $8**

BB-154 **"Space Walrus" Kevin L. Donihe** — Walter is supposed to go where no walrus has ever gone before, but all this astronaut walrus really wants is to take it easy on the intense training, escape the chimpanzee bullies, and win the love of his human trainer Dr. Stephanie. **160 pages $11**

BB-155 **"Unicorn Battle Squad" Kirsten Alene** — Mutant unicorns. A palace with a thousand human legs. The most powerful army on the planet. **192 pages $11**

BB-156 **"Kill Ball" Carlton Mellick III** — In a city where all humans live inside of plastic bubbles, exotic dancers are being murdered in the rubbery streets by a mysterious stalker known only as Kill Ball. **134 pages $10**

BB-157 **"Die You Doughnut Bastards" Cameron Pierce** — The bacon storm is rolling in. We hear the grease and sugar beat against the roof and windows. The doughnut people are attacking. We press close together, forgetting for a moment that we hate each other. **196 pages $11**

BB-158 **"Tumor Fruit" Carlton Mellick III** — Eight desperate castaways find themselves stranded on a mysterious deserted island. They are surrounded by poisonous blue plants and an ocean made of acid. Ravenous creatures lurk in the toxic jungle. The ghostly sound of crying babies can be heard on the wind. **310 pages $13**

BB-159 **"Thunderpussy" David W. Barbee** — When it comes to high-tech global espionage, only one man has the balls to save humanity from the world's most powerful bastards. He's Declan Magpie Bruce, Agent 00X. **136 pages $11**

BB-160 **"Papier Mâché Jesus" Kevin L. Donihe** — Donihe's surreal wit and beautiful mind-bending imagination is on full display with stories such as All Children Go to Hell, Happiness is a Warm Gun, and Swimming in Endless Night. **154 pages $11**

BB-161 **"Cuddly Holocaust" Carlton Mellick III** — The war between humans and toys has come to an end. The toys won. **172 pages $11**

BB-162 **"Hammer Wives" Carlton Mellick III** — Fish-eyed mutants, oceans of insects, and flesh-eating women with hammers for heads. Hammer Wives collects six of his most popular novelettes and short stories. **152 pages $10**